Amazon Angel

Prose Series 6

Yolande Villemaire

Amazon Angel

**Translated from the French
by Gérald Leblanc**

Guernica

Montreal/New York, 1993

Copyright © Yolande Villemaire and Les Herbes Rouges, 1982.
Translation © by Guernica Editions Inc. and Gérald Leblanc, 1993.
All rights reserved.
Typeset and printed in Canada.
Cover conception: Julia Gualtieri.

Antonio D'Alfonso, editor.
Guernica Editions Inc.
P.O. Box 633, Station N.D.G.
Montreal (Quebec), Canada H4A 3R1

Guernica Editions Inc.
340 Nagel Drive
Cheektowaga, N.Y. 14225-4731 USA

The publisher gratefully acknowledges financial
assistance from The Canada Council and
Le ministère des Affaires culturelles du Québec

The publisher would like to thank Pasquale
Verdicchio for his editorial suggestions.

Legal Deposit – First Quarter
National Library of Canada and Bibliothèque nationale du Québec.

Canadian Cataloguing in Publication Data
Villemaire, Yolande
[Ange amazone. English]
Amazon Angel

(Prose series; 6)
ISBN 0-920717-20-9

I. Title II. Title: Ange amazone. English. III. Series.

PS8593.I39A813 1993   C843'.54   C91-090603
PQ3919.2.V44A813 1993

For Gabrielle Roth

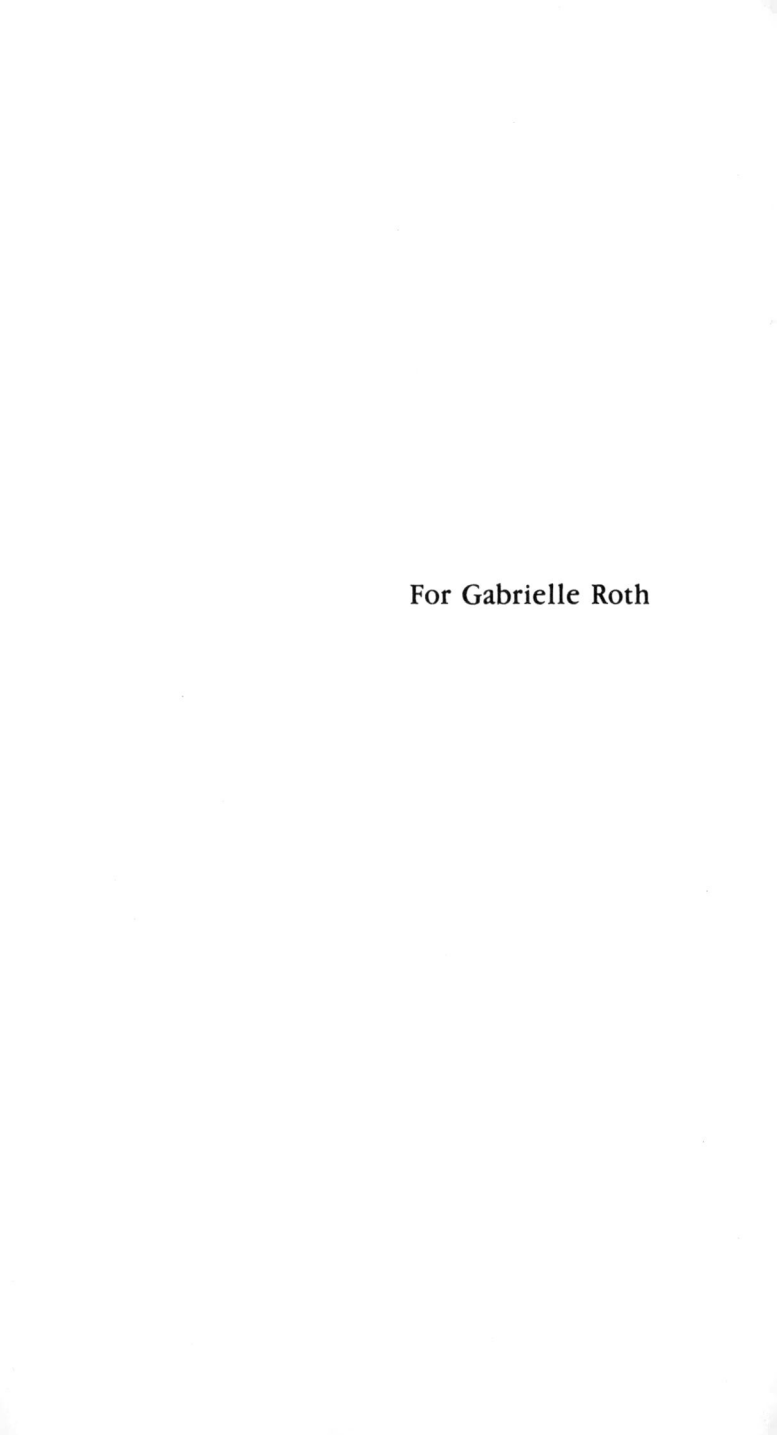

I

Lucifer, Lucifer, for the Beauty of the Devil, I Would Even Go Down to Hell

I remember the sun, red, between the palms of my hands open in the double mudra. I recall the fire of his breath on my forehead. Memory returns, Estelle, memory returns.

The sun rises from the east at Maui as at Molokai, at Kauai as at Oahu, at Lanai as at Hawaii. The sun rises from the east, I swear, Estelle, I swear to you. I have seen it with my own two eyes. Standing in front of the black lunar crater of Haleakala, I am the god Maui staring at the sun in the lasso of my gaze. I stop his course in the sky. Sun, deliver us from time. Sun, illuminate us.

Shaman, my love, you are beating the drum and I close my eyes on the fiery veil of passion. As I burn fear, you rhyme my descent into hell. Drum beat pulses in the master heart of my right hand, holding my left hand. I cross my closed fists on my shoulders in the courage mudra.

The sun is already much higher in the sky. Clouds heaped over the cold mouth of the mauve crater rise in phantasmic columns, catch fire. Standing on a rock, Raphael the archangel, inspired by devas, plays the flute while Amazon angels, androgynes armed with cymbals, triangles, and small bells, strike up a hymn to the sun, much to the displeasure of early morning tourists wondering what these freaks are up to.

I unfold my arms, and that is when I meet your eyes, shaman, my love, always beating the drum. Ah Lucifer, Lucifer, the dark fever in your pupils. Lucifer, Lucifer, beautiful fallen angel remembering heaven. He is dancing in your eyes, shaman, my love, to the rhythm of the drum. He dances in your eyes, he dances in my body. Lucifer, angel of light, grabs me, Estelle, and I scream, to the rhythm of the drum: '*There is a beast in the beat. There is a beast in the beat. There is a beast in the beat.*'*

While I surrender to Lucifer the Dance at the altitude of ten thousand feet on a volcano in the middle of the Pacific, the memory of the red race of Atlantis awakens in me. I am frightened, Estelle, I am frightened. I am a daughter of fire and desire, I burn and I blaze; I am a dragon, Estelle. I spit the fire of my swallowed rage, still

---

*The English phrases that are in italics throughout this translation appear in English in the original text (translator's note).

frightened to go through the fire. Ten million witches burnt alive, and as many cats howl in my painful memory. I want the fire, Estelle, I want it. I want the panting passion of fire when it gallops through sugar cane on the night-blue backdrop, the Maui sky.

Who is that little girl in white up there, left of my night? I turn my head towards her. She smiles in profile against the sky-velvet indigo. I recognize her. It is the little girl on the Christmas card I sent you, Estelle. Do you remember her ermine-lined white coat, her swan-feathered hat, her little white boots, the lilies she is holding in her hands, her white wings softly folded under the flurries? It is the snow maiden in Joseph Cornell's collage smiling at me from up there, way up, to the left. How did she escape the New York Museum of Modern Art, Estelle? How did she get out of the Christmas card and fasten herself like so on the azure backdrop of a dream? She is waving to me, calling me.

I am trembling, Estelle. I am a small white maiden shivering in flurries under the sky's weight. If I close my eyes and dream, I dream I dreamt that I was falling in a hallway of blue objects. It is a tube of light sweeping time and colouring in blue the points of intersection of my dreams. The kitten of my childhood turns blue with rage and becomes a sympathetic little diplodocus, its spine burning with a succession of blue fires. It turns slightly towards me. I pick it up in my arms, remembering the pilot of propane gas lit under the floor of that house, a blue mosque in Cairo. I am walking on the beach in spongy Albanian shoes. A man in a suit emerges from black-blue water, while a cardboard house inscribed with *Acadie* sinks slowly like a shipwreck. Apples are blue in the wet tree, like little verdigris angel tears. I am wearing an Iranian jewel around my neck: a white half-moon framed in blue ceramic cubes on a black string. I have forgotten my blue suitcase. I am a funny-looking spy in my blue cotton Chinese kimono, but I fly with ease between the towers of Place de la Cité and over Montreal, city of cobalt and cyanide, turquoise sunflower city in the blue iris of archangel memory.

I am frightened, Estelle. I am frightened because I am only a small snow maiden in a hypermnesic state; I do not want to drown in the heavy, profound blue waves of my other lives. Our little life is but a dream. *Our little life is but a dream rounded with some sleep.*

Our little life is but a dream rounded with some sleep. I am looking at the shining tips of my black boots. I am wearing a long black dress, a black and white head-dress, round glasses in gold metal frames. This is China, around 1910. In the north of China. Near T'ien-Tsin. In autumn. The distant mountains are red and yellow. It feels like autumn, cool, and yet it is only August. Across the river, the coolies are getting ready to leave. The Chinese guide is explaining something to me in Chinese, but I am looking at the red and yellow mountains and my spirit takes off, my mind wanders, takes refuge a few feet above my body, oh not too high, at level with the horizon. All of a sudden, I know I have been here before. For thirty years, I have been a missionary in China under the pretext of Christian charity when, in fact, it is only out of curiosity that I wanted to come here, to China, where I have lived in a previous life. It is almost funny.

I was born in the New Hebrides in 1853 and went through my novitiate in Australia. My name is Mother of Mercy. I speak Chinese fluently. I have waited fifty-seven years to experience this moment of clarity and doubt. If I am certain of having already lived in China, I am no less certain of being Catholic and not believing in reincarnation like the Buddhists. But it is a nice day and I want to laugh. I come back to our conversation. And then I notice that the young Oriental is very handsome; I burst out laughing. He too laughs, as we set out across a little wooden bridge. It is a nice day, the air is cool, the mountains are red and yellow on the horizon.

It is spring, two years later. Having set up the new school, I am tired. I trace a character on the blackboard and turn around. How naughty is the little one. As ugly as a mouse, with his hair in a brushcut. I am tired. The children are expecting a reprimand. I look outside, at the fresh green-mossed leaves on the trees. I am really quite tired.

1919. I have a fever. I am hot, I am cold. It is spring, maybe summer. I am in bed, in a white tent. My hair is wet, my nightdress is wet. I am weak, very weak. It is tuberculosis. In the afternoon, through an opening in the tent, a white bird, slender on its feet, enters. It oscillates its head, coos, shows me its brilliant left eye, very brilliant. Its feathers are very, very white, milky. I look at it, tell myself that it is the Holy Ghost. I feel like laughing, but no longer have the strength. At night, I cannot sleep. All night I see this afternoon's bird in the center of my mind. I am alone. In the dark. I am weak, very weak. Of course, it is the Holy Ghost. From the opening in the tent, it is grey. My head is on the pillow and yet I see the white bird enter, jumping on its skinny legs. I must be dreaming. But no, the bird has flown to my hands. I feel its light weight on my left hand. My hands are joined on my chest. The Holy Ghost has come to rest on me. I lift my left hand lightly to see the bird, but it flies away. A shame! It was not the Holy Ghost... That is when I die. In a single breath. I am floating above my bed. I am very tall, very thin, my hair is long and white. I am soaked, and so are the bedsheets. Outside, to the right, there is a ceremony. A priest in a purple chasuble. Prayer mills, banners. I do not know what it is. It may be my burial. Like a bird in flight, I fly over Australia, a heap of dark green in the blue Pacific. I do not come down again. I go up. I rise on ascending air to that black and blue planet from which emerges a blue and black light that makes me spin at breakneck speed. When Mother pours liquid bluing in the washing machine, it spins like that, like a whirlpool.

I have black crocodile shoes, black nylon stockings, a black-laced slip. I am adjusting a black silk flower in my hair. It is afternoon. The curtains are drawn. Heavy beige drapes, rose-tinted. It is Paris, 1940. My name is Celia. I am standing behind a black-lacquered Chinese folding screen. A rainbow stands out in relief against the black-blue clouds. He is still asleep. I feel good in my body. Happy. He is blond, he may be German. Maybe not. It may not be the first time. I am twenty years old, and I have made love all afternoon. It does not seem as though there is a war going on. I am slipping into a Chinese-style kimono dress. It is black and white, very pretty. My perfume is wonderful. I am a bit drowsy.

1946. A river, grey. A grey day. Boredom. Forgetfulness. I only know the little snow maiden trembling from sadness in front of the boundlessness of the sky at Maui. It is then that the angel appears, the prodigious archangel, big as the sky. The pleats of his blue velvet dress fall from the boundlessness of sky, while the archangel bends over and picks up the little snow maiden in his arms. Is it you, archangel Gabriel, or is it you, Estelle? Is it you shaman, my love, who holds me close to your heart and flies away to the right of the sky to show me ten thousand suns turning, red and yellow, eggs sunny side up in the clear blue heavens? It is a bit like Disneyland here, the angels' Marineland. I really love the aerial view from your arms, my angel. But why have you forgotten China and Japan? They are as important as the amusement park. You are a high school teacher? Oh well! I find the driving slower in this taxi. Yes, this numbness in my hands, the doctor said it was a neurological disorder. What do you think, *mon ange?* Do you also think that it is a question of pinched cervical vertebrae? The taxi driver turns around and says that it is my healing power that causes the tingling in my hands.

Do you remember, Estelle, the letter I wrote you last year in which I told you about my trip through the Parc des Laurentides on the day of the first snow? That old woman on the bus, on the verge of having a heart attack. Do you remember the improvised wild gesturing that I went through? I have just learned that I had, that day, unknowingly massaged the master of the heart. No doubt an old acupuncture memory coming back through the mists of time. I am hurting, Estelle. I am hurting so much.

My jaw is as hard as cement, firmly closed on the red octopus of my rage. I am a caged fawn in my body, bruised by thought-forms travelling in time, through electric and telephone wires. I am crossed with wires and mental spaces that confuse and diffuse my mind, that pull on my muscles, that bend and twist my nerves. I have facial neuralgia, as though I have just been slapped. Yes, put your hands of fire once again on my face, archangel Michael. Press your fingers on my bones, make the fire penetrate the hardened mask of my terror and pain. Let me moan with my eyes closed to the orange rays projecting from your hands as they feel and mold my face. I try very hard to fix in time-space this changing face like a sky of wind and storm. I surrender it to the heat of your hands. Let the red marks of the devil be erased, let the violet cleansing flame arise.

And, while the archangel Michael's sword of blue light presides over this exotic sunrise, my mind leaps in time. Stretched out on three seats in a half-empty Boeing 747, halfway between Honolulu and Los Angeles, I let my lukewarm tears wash away my sadness. I roll myself up in an American Airlines' red blanket and listen to the music on the headphones. I see the devil. He is tall, big, and brown. He looks like the Minotaur with his horns and red rags. To the right, Michael the archangel rips the screen with his sword of blue light. To his right, the archangel Gabrielle, disguised as an orange dragonfly ballerina, bows. To her left, the archangel Raphael, in burgundy-coloured robe, stands on his boulder, conducting a choir of angels. To the extreme left of Satan, the archangel Gabriel, in a black chapel, is lovingly rolfing the knots in my body. I weep. I weep because it is so good. The devil carries me in his arms, as we take the elevator. King Kong and his prey are descending in the chthonian regions of the mind.

A hundred stories below, the elevator stops. I leave the cage, the doors close on Satan who apparently goes up again. A Navajo Indian waits for me. Or Huichol. It is in the American desert. Everything is red. It may be Colorado. The man looks a bit aged, small, muscled. He sports long black tresses. He motions me to follow him. It is foggy. We cross a wooden bridge that oscillates in the fog. We wander into the red rock mountains. After about fifteen minutes, we come upon an old man in a white tunic. He is wearing a turban and a white beard. His skin is pink, he is chubby faced. I understand that I have been brought to God. I find this pleasant but I am still somewhat intimidated. Then God ascends, levitates, rises like a helium balloon. He stabilizes at ten feet from the ground, opens his tunic in a vaguely obscene gesture, shows his pink nylon stockings, his garter belt and his flesh-tone bra. At this point, I recognize Severo Sarduy and I burst out laughing.

The sun rises again above Haleakala crater. The whole sky catches fire. It is the first dawn of time. Memory returns, Estelle, memory returns. Amazon angel, androgyne, hear the red howl of my senses and consume me in your violet flame. I go forward through *the black ocean of reality*, a young white woman always absent, heavy with archetypes, encumbered by my six pairs of wings, for I am Michael, Raphael, Gabriel and, Lucifer, Lucifer, for the beauty of the devil, I would even go down to hell, I am Lucifer. I come forward, Amazon angel, androgyne, my nape pierced by a kryptonite green laser ray. I come forward, a young white woman always absent in the blackness of the dark memory of Egypt and all the red races. I sing the green laser ray with a frog in my throat. I sing from whence I come. In that green light from asteroid 823 that we call krypton in the geography book of Clark Kent and Superman. Amazon angel, androgyne, *can you read my mind? Can you read my mind?* Sing the pink sound that heals the pain that *will come again and again and again.* Amazon angel, androgyne, I come forward through *the black ocean of reality* in your aura of orange amarilla, my mauve gaze drowned in stardust tears. The green laser beam of memory pierces through me and it looks like fear, but Amazon angel, androgyne, come through, I have no choice. I have no choice, under the blue sky.

I walk on earth in the body of earth. Amazon angel, androgyne, do not stay pinned like a night butterfly in the heart of night. You can close your arms and take the green laser ray of kryptonite in your hands to open *the black ocean of reality*, Amazon angel, androgyne. With your hair on fire, under the blue sky, under the black of the black exactly under the sun, under the star-spangled vault, under the rainbows, you come forward from the bottom of a crater miles and thousands of miles from here. I know you are coming forward, Amazon angel, androgyne, that you are coming forward like a rainbow towards Atlantis. *Can you read my mind, Estelle, can you read my mind? Estrella del camino real, donde está usted, Miguel?*

II
Orange

Noon on the beach at Haena. I bite into a mango. Miguel would say: *'La vida está mango mango!'* Far, very far in time and space. Fruit juice splashes my aloe-coated thighs. Orange thighs on coral sand. I roll naked on the beach, coating myself with mango-sand in the pink conch at noon on the beach at Haena. Nobody. I flow naked in azure water, malachite, tender. *Agua caliente*, as in his language. I am alone at the other end of the world, Valentina, thousands and thousands of miles from him, and I miss his body. I flow back to the rhythm of the waves, on the border between the sand and the sea. I open my eyes on the salt, the blue of the sky, the orange crackling of noon, and I yearn for Miguel. How many millions of bodies between him and me at this moment? How many millions of bodies on this island alone? Still there is no one else here. It is mine. Naked as a mussel, bivalve, pulsing, refulgent, I curl and I spiral, liquid Venus lying in the lukewarm water of the Pacific, listening to the sound of the sea.

The sun seeps into the lips of my sex, licks my stomach, my breasts. I hallucinate:

the copper skin of Miguel, his weight, his desire, the thumping of his solar plexus in my soul when he makes love to me. I yearn to bite in the blackness of his hair, but it is salt that I taste when I swallow a mouthful of the Pacific. Ah Valentina, Valentina, to see Haena and to die of desire in the swelling surf.

I swim under transparent water, towards the high sea. Small, bright yellow fish dart around me. Before me, a black coral wall. I stick my head out of the water, breathe in hungrily. Lying face-down on the reef, I look at the sea soaping up, white and aquamarine, at the horizon. I turn on my back and contemplate the intense blue, the perfect blue of the Kaui sky. It is still noon. I am in paradise, and yet my whole body anticipates that moment when, thousands and thousands of miles from here, I will merge with him in an opalescent skin of silk. Honey, red clover, orange blossom water – how I miss the smell of him, the smell of him! Ah Valentina, Valentina, to see seeing and die of tenderness in a heartbeat!

I dive into turquoise water the colour of precious stones and swim to the beach. A thin rain lightly begins. Grey curtains of moisture slide on the shuddering sea. I shiver from joy and cold under the sting of tiny needles. It is raining hard now, teasing my eyes. I am drunk with hoary water. Suddenly weary, I put on my Hawaiian cotton-wool sweater, the lower part of my bikini, and start walking.

My knapsack is too heavy. Walking barefoot in this sand is difficult. It is raining very hard. Everything has darkened. Clouds flow along the harshness of the Na Pali beach. The trees turn forest-green, drawing the whole beach towards mauve. I did not expect it to be cold in paradise.

Like a blow to the heart, the sun comes out, explodes, chasing the gloom away. The sky moves quickly, a fast cinematographic image. Mauve rises in cloudy masses and, blessed miracle, a rainbow falls through the dewy shower.

It is then that you appear, Valentina. Sitting in a lotus position on the orange beach, there, exactly where the rainbow ends. Your amber-rose hair shines like solar gold, your eyes are closed, and you smile. You smile like Demeter herself must smile when she tastes the fruits of the earth. It is only an image of you, Valentina, a light-year image, the crystallized form of your mind. But when I stop, mute, several feet from the goddess, her eyes open and I fall from vertigo into her mauve pupils, iridescent with stars.

I see the phantom ship of my dreams, a pink and grey Arachnid ship, a jumble of ropes and tacks, lines and webs tied to the great masts that oscillate from the wind that blows strongly through it all, forcing, ringing, clinking, jingling through this paper hardware. This ship is merely a holograph scrim on a lake at Deux-Montagnes that is itself a thin film of cellophane. I could peel it off to see what lies behind it and then fall off the earth. Ah Valentina, you look so very real, and yet I lose sight of you. You are but a tiny dot on the immense Hanalei beach at Haena. I run away with the wind, perched on the highest mast of my phantom ship. Its pink sails snap, split and flap like wandering souls around the black yard. I thought I had misled, lost, buried her years ago, the shadow in a red cape coming forward walking on the waves. Her blood-red nails, her vampish appearance, her reddish hair. Ah Valentina, the sanguinary smell, the sanguinary glow of this red woman of interior tombs and dungeons. Marrakesh-the-red rises from the blood bath of my memory and slowly comes forward on my phantom ship that sails, practically flies, on the violet waters of the high seas. She comes so close that I can smell her wine-stained breath. She puts her hands on my shoulders. I close my eyes and cry. I struggle in the dark,

Valentina. I am under the spell of the succubus of Lethe who murmurs: 'Forget my dear, forget.' But I howl with rage in my blank memory, I become unruly, I sing at the top of my lungs: *'I've been told I've been talking all night with a can of tomato juice.'* I sing from the throat, from the head; I sing anything, I am a fire siren. She slaps me. Very simply, she slaps me. I look straight into her eyes. And I see. I see that it is me. My shadow, Hecate, Kali-magician, woman of Egypt and shade. I was frightened by my shadow. And I fall into the fire of her eyes.

Yellow. Glaucous. It is not a nice yellow. I cannot see yet, I am a newborn child. I am being carried, rocked in a baby carriage. I am not happy here. I am three-and-a-half months old. I am in a crib, watching the red and white squares of the dirty floor. The bedroom door is open, it has yellowed. This is Paris. I can see the clay-tiled roofs. There is a calendar on the wall. It says: *1850.* That is the date of my death. It will be a while. I hear them screaming. My mother and her husband. His name is Gabriel, a sailor. He hates me. Because I am not his daughter. She had me when he was away. He screams that he is going to kill me. I hate him too. I have known him for a long time. I have hated him for a long time. My name is Sélanie Sue. I'm five years old and I am in distress. In big, big distress, I am in bondage, in the darkness. They've been hiding me since I've been born 'cause I'm not supposed to have been born. I'm afraid in the dark, and bored. But there's a moon in the window. The moon is white, is round, is beautiful. It throws light in my room. Sometimes there's a dog at the window across the way, a nice beige dog that barks. But now, nothing. And I cry.

My face is sore. He's tied me to a chair and he's slapping me because I don't want to speak. It hurts, it hurts, it hurts. My head swings from one side to the other. I clench my teeth. He says he'll make me talk, goddam little bastard. He says he wants to kill me. My mother cries.

There's a little girl in the kitchen. Her mother is holding her by the shoulder. This lady is a friend of my mother's. She's wearing a long grey coat. The little girl has her eyes closed. She's really, really beautiful. She has her eyes closed, and she's smiling. It's the first time that I see her. My mother says her name's Amélie, and we're going to keep her. She has short dark hair and her skin is white, white. All of a sudden, she opens her eyes. They're blue! She's so beautiful, I love her! She smiles.

Amélie and I are in my room. I'm looking out the window. Amélie is trying to draw the street because I've never seen it at ground level. Amélie says she'll try to draw it to show me what it's like.

I have to go to the bathroom. I look at the tips of my black booties. I wanna pee. I have black stockings, a black wool dress. I'm seven years old. They've locked me up in my room. I know what they're doing. I've been locked up for a long time. I have to go to the bathroom.

It stinks. I'm crouched in a corner, behind the door. I've peed on the floor. I've been locked up for two days. It stinks, it's yellow. I knock on the door, I scream, I cry. Why have they locked me up for so long? I'm hungry. It's as if they weren't there. It's as if they were dead. I'm going to lie down on my bed and die.

Something carries me down. Someone is carrying me in their arms. Down the staircase. THE STAIRCASE! I'm going to see the street, I'm going to see the street! We get to the street. It's spinning, it's grey, it's high. The pavement is also grey.

I'm thirty-eight years old, I'm drunk. I hold my bottle of red wine and laugh hard enough to split my face open. The bells are ringing. It's a Sunday morning, sunny. I've found the first street of my life. I had wanted to see the street so much that now I live here. There are two other older people with me. They're laughing but they don't understand. I still won't speak.

I'm lying on my side in bed. I'm in a home. They think I'm crazy. But I'm not crazy at all. There's a black crucifix above the door of the dormitory. They can go to hell with their God. There's never been any God for me!

A doctor is taking my pulse. There's a meat-like smell. I peek over the sheets at a nurse coming up the row of beds with her carriage and her pot of meat soup. A skinny old man screams.

There is a nun looking at me. She has pinched lips and looks disgusted. I place a bottle of red wine in my head and send it into her head. I don't think the suggestion is going to work. Not long after, she brings me my bottle. She must have felt sorry for me. I drink and I laugh.

Someone is holding my left wrist. My face is sore. There is something heavy on my face, it hurts. It's a mask. A golden mask, it's surely the first time I've seen gold.

It is the Mayan mask of god-alcohol. Yellow. Gold. I am locked in a golden sarcophagus floating above my sick bed. The sarcophagus rises over Paris, straightens up, stands, and is propelled in darkness at full speed between the rows of Egyptian and Inca mummies.

I am barefoot, tired and half asleep, I am sitting on a beach, my back against a cliff. A coconut tree bends over me. I am very, very tired. My wife is coming along the beach with the youngest child. She is wearing a red pareu. He is handsome, little Maleko. He is not mine, it shows, but I love the little one. More than I have ever loved the four others. He is still small, a skinny and curly-headed baby, he laughs all the time. He is leaning on my wife's shoulders. I take him from her and carry him in my arms.

My wife has left. I have laid the little one beside me in the sand. Like a small animal, he clings to my chest. I see something in the water. It is big, huge. A whale? It comes out of the water, grey metal, moving forward on the sand. I get up quickly with the little one. It disappears before my eyes. I do believe that I am much too tired. I lie down again with the little one.

I am in the mouth of my great-grandmother. She is pulling on her mouth. It hurts. She is in the hut. The one I now inhabit with my mother, my wife, and my five children. I am in the mouth of my long-dead great-grandmother looking at the white rectangular light on the ceiling.

I wake up in the hut beside my wife. The sun is rising. I cling to her. I see the entrance to a grotto, a staircase of black stone. It becomes a spinning well of darkness and I moan that it is endless, endless. My wife holds me in her arms. Thank God, she's there. My whole body aches. I have the impression that spirits are working in my flesh, that I am becoming human. My wife says I should admit that I am called to become the shaman. I do not want our race to become extinct, yet I know that the white man is coming.

I am walking on the beach and I feel the weird attraction of the shamanic call. I am like a woman in labour, I dance in my brown frog body. Hundreds of brown frogs leap on the humid sand around me. I see the soul of an ancestor howling in the wind of the coconut tree shaking in the moonlight. I hear the hissing of flying fish.

Hissing, hushing sounds in the silence after the rain. I turn toward the sea, a school of flying fish passes in gliding flight on the edge of the water. When I turn towards you, Valentina, you are holding your hands in the sacred love mudra.

The wind has chased the last clouds away. I remove my wet sweater and sit naked in front of you. I do the sacred love mudra. It is then that the phantom ship of my dream appears between your hands. It is an exact replica, all the complicated gear is there, and even the exact shades of pink and grey of the dreamlike object. How did you do it, Valentina? It is a perfect hologram flickering with light, an expert visualisation entirely materialized, how did you do it, Valentina, how did you do it?

You answer that there is no wizardry to it. You read my dream when it passed through my mind. You say 'There', and the rest I can see. You see the Arachnid ship, as it sails in my eyes. You capture it on your retina. You go down the pearl-spiralled stairway, jumping and dancing, and sing softly: *'Which one is real, which one is real. Both are real, yes both are real.'* It is your password. You find yourself in front of your black office door in New York. You ring. The blue Oriental from the starchbox who works as your secretary comes to answer. He greets you obsequiously, and invites you to enter your high-tech office with the sparkling red floor under your yellow work table and green chair. The filing cabinet is orange, the lamp ultra-violet, and the crystal ball aquamarine. In front of you, on a giant screen, New York is glowing with lights. You put on your sunglasses, and you say 'Chang' – because the Chinese boy is evidently named Chang – you say 'Chang, please show my advisors in, please.' Chang manoeuvres a venetian blind and Gene Kelly emerges in white flannel pants and a light white wool sweater. He does a few steps and then gallantly kisses your hand. You kiss him on the mouth, as usual, and on the neck, staining the collar of his white silk shirt with your cherry-red lipstick which will disintegrate in thirty seconds. You say: 'Well, where is Isadora?' She falls into your arms, breathless, dizzy, delighted and delightful in her black-sequined dress.

Isadora Duncan is fragrant with the essence of lilies of the valley, a scent that always turns your head. Your advisors seize the moment and exchange a screen kiss of elevating passion until you finally succeed in interrupting them with the force of your nervous coughing. Finally, faces pink with excitement, and anxious to find out what delicate mission you are about to confer upon them, Isadora and Gene turn towards you. You then clearly expose the details of the problem: the date, the hour, the exact number, the seven figures of the number, the IBM code. You dim the superb view of New York to project on a giant screen the image captured by your retina. In this case, my phantom ship. Isadora nods, walks back and forth, rubbing her chin. Gene sits in the lotus position and immediately rises six inches off the ground, his eyes rolling upwards. You snap your fingers. Chang brings the lemon Perrier served in a Bohème crystal champagne flute glass.

Responding to another snap of the fingers, your two advisors start talking simultaneously. In their mixed verbiage, you gather the essentials: the three hundred and sixty-five fundamental pieces of data to program your holographic machine, in order to reproduce exactly the mental image of my little ship. As your advisors, tired out by their cogitations, fall wrapped together on the red and uncomfortable tiles of your New York office, you snap your fingers a third time. Chang activates a lever, and, like a goddess-of-the-machine, Valentina II descends from the ceiling in the pink spray of fireworks. The luminous sphere stands still at your height. After having made your last recommendations to Chang for the upkeep of your New York office during your absence, and after your silent farewell to Isadora Duncan and Gene Kelly who, respectively, snore and smile in their dreams, you finally settle at the control of your super flying machine.

In a short time, you are flying over Montreal, city of red lights and hematite, scarlet sunflower city in the bloody eyes of a lethal red-skin.

Ah Valentina, Valentina, to see seeing and die holographed! It is then that, between the hissing of two schools of flying fish, you say that I can. You say that I can and then you say nothing more.

I say 'I can?' and I do not know what. You do not say anything. I know that I can and I do not know what. I cry on the beach at Haena. Imperturbably, you do not say anything.

Later, on the 12:25 Dash-Express between the Lihue airport at Kaui and Honolulu at Oahu, I will see you bend over the porthole. Valentina. And, seeing you look from high above the SS Arizona memorial, I will see the hologram of Pearl Harbor, December 7th 1941, materialize in my hands.

III

The Map Will Never Be the Territory

The Diamond Head sparkles in the setting, scale-like sun. I have the feeling that I could be sad, Iris. My pain is an amber pearl recalled in the oyster heart. I nibble on the sky. My sadness is a frightened puma in a cage.

I sense I could engrave the glorious image of the sun on the Diamond Head in my mind. I feel the quality of light at this moment flickers eternally in my consciousness. And I am sad, Iris, because already night falls on Waikiki Beach, and the Diamond Head is only a sequined shadow in my mind.

I am writing to you from the terrace of Hau Tree Lanai, under the banyan tree which, according to the menu, was celebrated by Stevenson. I have just passed one hour and many quarters playing an extraordinary Japanese electronic game. It is a labyrinth of luminous dots that a yellow mouth, controlled by the player, must devour. As soon as the signal is given, the three guardians – red, pink and powder blue – relentlessly pursue the yellow mouth. Unless it can gobble one of the four white points on time, the guardian will swallow it. When absorbed, the points colour the guardians in deep blue, making them strangely vulnerable to the devouring yellow mouth. The game consists of the yellow mouth swallowing the blue guardians for two hundred, three hundred, four hundred points, before they regain their colour and their aggressiveness. It is quite an art to get the yellow mouth to move and swallow, before it is swallowed! But it always ends up being swallowed since, of course, the game has an end.

I have the feeling that I am living as if I will die any day now. As if one has to have a reason to be sad. I watch* the gold and orange haloed sun sink in the Pacific. The clouds fluff, pink and blue, beneath the horizon line. This sky is so beautiful, Iris, that I do not want to see it change. The beauty of the sky, though, comes from the fact that it passes above our heads, always the same sky, and yet never the same. I was about to read the future in the beard of Proteus, when suddenly that beard frayed in white routes meandering in the clearing, lapis lazuli sky of Waikiki.

It is as when you sing, Iris, the blue waves make all those tears fall softly from your eyes to your mouth, giving your tears the aura of galaxies which forever drop and rise, up to Ariel, your soul the Holy Ghost. It is as when you dance a tragic tango, shaman, my friend, and let yourself go to the sobbing rhythms that shake you, in the middle of a ballroom, where everyone does Tai Chi. *Blue, blue, blue, lost in the blue*, you twirl about with a melancholic smile, shaman, my friend. Your spleen is a tango, a two-steps, a pavane, a saltarello.

Glissé, jeté, glissé, jeté: your legs draw strange patterns on the floor. You do an about-turn, whirl with your semaphore arms. You roll your shoulders, shaman, my friend, you roll your eyes, your hips, you bend your wrists. It is a belly dance of the suffering, shaman, my friend, my dance master.

I am so sad, Iris. How not to be sad when there is so much hunger and misery in the world; the neutron bomb, cancer, the war. So much thoughtlessness and mine, Iris, mine too. My powerlessness.

Venus rises in the royal-blue sky of six o'clock in the evening, I think I am able to see the celestial will glimmering at a distance. But I am sad, Iris, not knowing how to penetrate the mystery. So I forget about it. I drink my pineapple juice and feel like a really small, white clown, juggling brilliant theories, universal remedies, all the while walking a tightrope under the big top.

The waves roll blue towards the shore. It looks as though there are reefs about thirty feet from the shore, the waves rise there regularly. Yet, there are none. I swam there this afternoon, and there weren't any! Looking closely, I see a fin, then a second, and finally, a dolphin leaps from the water. It is a school of dolphins capering about in the dusk. I am no longer sad, Iris. I am tempted to follow them in their game. They cross the Honolulu Bay where the skyscrapers glow. The lights that run through the branches of the giant banyan tree on the terrace light up, multicoloured. A waiter ignites torches suspended over the beach.

Earlier, while paying for my drink, I took Azélie Zee Artand's miniature road map from my wallet, the one you gave me before my departure. My hand touches the magic credit card that teaches me how to follow the movement of my passion. On one side, the word *étrangère* sticks out. A rose, cut in two, stands out on pink ecoline to the left of this mental insurance card. A red diagonal line crosses it at several millimeters to the right of its centre. It is there that we find the word *étrangère* in black lettraset on an orange ecoline background. I read my desire to descend into my body,

Iris, and to cross the red line of interdiction that makes me a stranger to myself, cut in two, confined to half-measures, and cleaved. On the other side, a postage stamp. It reads *New Guinea*. A black woman smiles under her thick, electric hair. She looks happy, in spite of the long golden needles stuck in her face. The heavy gold necklace she wears is obliterated by the black waves of the postmark. Traced in ecoline, orange waves pulsate through her face, run across it disappearing, open pseudopods branching out on the white vertigo of the other side of the card. Two number sevens, one on one side, the other on the back, float on the stream of colour. *'I will get you back into the flow,'* she seems to say under her thin plasticized coat.

'I will get you back into the flow,' as you were telling me, shaman, my friend: when lost in the hologram of my desires, I forget to follow my feet and see up to where they lead me.

I have patent leather shoes, white socks. The sky is blue, the stars big and silvery. I am two years old, huddled in a Christmas crib.

My feet are bare under the white sheets. I am dying. I am called Gontran. A little girl about eight years old is standing at my feet, her hand on the knob of the open door. She is wearing white clothing, ribbons of brown velvet in her dark hair. She looks at me. She is my granddaughter, my daughter's child. She is the only one in this house who loves me. I try to speak to her. I ready my lips to speak, but I can barely move them. I would like to say something but the sounds do not come. I moan.

Near my bed, to the left, a nun is praying. A priest in a dark soutane manipulates a monstrance above me. I turn my head towards them. It is snowing outside the window. It is dark. Yet it is only one o'clock in the afternoon.

During the night, I try to recall my granddaughter well, so that I can bring her face with me in death. I do not want to forget her.

In the morning, screams. My daughter is giving birth to another child. I understand. I suddenly feel I understand. Life, death. Love. I love my granddaughter. I would like to talk to her, touch her tiny hand. She is no longer at the door. But I remember her. It is the first time in my whole life that I have felt something like this. Love... I have always been considered simple-minded. And I have believed them. I have hated them. I am dying and I realize that I can understand. My mind is clear as it has never been. I see the image of my granddaughter, standing in the doorway looking at me. A fleeting sadness. A look of distance. Because I am sounding a death rattle, she is a little scared of me now. But I will return, little one, I will return to guide you.

Unexpectedly, I breathe better. I see the snow at the window. Mountains of dazzling snow. I see my feet, my patent leather shoes, my white socks. The paper-blue sky, the silvery stars of the crib where I hid when I was two years old. The ending is like the beginning. It is not difficult to understand. My father and my mother are sitting in a sleigh with God. The snow is very, very white. Very, very white. Yellow. It is now yellow.

The sky is high, black, dotted with stars through the branches of the banyan tree. I look at the miniature road map in profile. It is a thin white line against the deep of the night. The red and green lights of a plane slide over my head. I let the map fall on the table: it shows its back or its front, who knows which is which. It shows its other side, the other side of the coin.

The tiger has followed us, I can hear it breathe heavily on the other side of the bamboo wall. My man licks my breasts, nibbles at them, while making small grunts. I massage the skull under his kinky hair. It feels so good to smell him again. I breathe in his smell. My man is back from Port Moresby. I missed him. The fire of desire rises, red, in my belly. We hold one another, wrapped, immobile, silent. The air is vibrant around our bodies. I kiss his mouth, his lips, his tongue, his teeth, his saliva, his smell. He licks my neck, my shoulders, my breasts, slides on my belly, penetrates my navel, wets it with saliva. He kisses my vulva, vibrates his tongue on my clitoris, spurting out juices. I want his penis that I hold long and hard in my hands. I lie down, he approaches, bends over me. Desire breathes in me, I moan. He slips his sex softly between my lips. I heave my hips, draw him into my vagina. He penetrates me, enlaces me, embraces me. My ears are on fire, my heart dilates, tears form in the corner of my eyes. He drinks them, massages my shoulders, my back, my buttocks. He penetrates further, hammers my belly, plunges and touches the wall of my matrix with his gland. I scream with pain and rapture. He slows down, I bounce under him. I am a tam-tam in the night and the rhythm takes me, intoxicates me, how good to be alive! His desire grows, fills me, opens me savagely; it is like he is rocking me at the same time. He gallops like a wild horse, I am ascending to heaven, his soul in my hands, I come in the earth body of my body, of his body, of the earth and of the night. He penetrates me and I receive him trembling, transfigured in a great white flash that welds me to him as he comes, sperm and sigh, volcano in my womb, ocean in my soul.

The pain tears my belly. I howl, grunt, sing the atrocious suffering that is labouring, my body undulating in childbirth. I am a disrupted land, chaos of flesh, brushing against the terror of my own birth, the boundary of my death. I search desperately for breath that pain takes away from me. I curse the day this child was conceived. I curse the heavens and the earth for allowing such suffering. For hours and hours and hours I give birth to this child who does not want to be born, clinging to my womb, desperately. This child is killing me.

I float above a hut on piles. It is the taboo hut, isolated from the village. It is dark. The moon is full in the indigo water of the lake. Milky. A blue dragon trembles on its white globe. Trembles and flaps its wings.

Honolulu sparkles on the night drop, now black, shimmering water and light in the mandala of my gaze. And I am sad, Iris, because the night is black, and I remember the light of the moon. I see again all the books in the Alexandrian library burning in the yellow flame of wisdom. All the books of Alexandria, Iris.

Jorge Luis Borges is sitting on a stool in the middle of the library of Babel in which all the shelves are covered with gold leaf and all the books gilt-edged. He is reading *Le Chercheur de trésors ou l'influence d'un livre* by Philippe Aubert de Gaspé fils. He is wondering why all these *Canadiens* hold this belief that one can possess all books, except one, as is indicated by a note at the bottom of the page. A whole section of the wall starts pivoting, revealing the cottage of Charles Amand. Walking on the tips of his toes, the Argentinian writer approaches the window of the alchemist furtively. The latter is reading *Le Petit Albert*, which is not surprising, since that is what he reads continuously. No, it is rather his striking resemblance to Séraphin Poudrier that leaves Jorge Luis flabbergasted, dumbfounded, kneeling below the window of Amand. But soon he says '*Porquè no? Porquè no?*' and he pursues his own sweet way in the labyrinth of the library of Babel, hyacinth and golden in the warm light of the world falling asleep.

Behind him, without his noticing, Charles Amand follows in his footsteps. Behind Charles Amand, Séraphin Poudrier. Finally, a few steps behind the miser, O.R., from *Un livre* by Nicole Brossard. Yellow dancing cloud, will-o'-the-wisp of memories intertwined and of mental mazes, O.R. hammers the ground with her feet and the whole building trembles. She is visibly having a great time, stealing a few books in passing. Following her, the golden child of Paul Chamberland. He walks with the solemnity of a communicant, his eyes fixed on an adamantine polyhedron vibrating with light in the hollow of his hands.

Borges turns around. The child is now holding the *ulak* diamond between his index finger and the thumb of his right hand. O.R. becomes more and more evanescent, until she disappears completely in the polyhedron. Séraphin Poudrier is transformed into a cloud and disappears in the same fashion. As for Charles Amand, he has turned around. Transfigured, he looks at the golden ray that aims right at his heart, snaps his resistance and transmutes him into photons. Borges keeps his good eye glued to the lethal ray. The golden child advances slowly toward him. The good eye of Borges is still resisting, a smooth and hard surface that returns and does not take. Having reached his height, the child looks into his eyes. Borges then asks him: '*Donde está el autobus para ir a El Dorado?*' Frightened, the child runs off into the maze.

On the plane between Maui and Oahu I doze off. In my possessed sleep, I see Don

Illan de Tolède appear with his books, his instruments of magic and witchcraft. I dream that Miguel is his sorcerer's apprentice, that he becomes a professor of mathematics, a nuclear physician and astrophysicist, a Nobel Prize winner for biology, and all of this is but a trick of Borges sitting on the steps of the cathedral of Buenos Aires.

I momentarily contemplate the whipped cream clouds above the Pacific as I return to Montreal, metropolis of black gold and bronze, daffodil city on the other end of the world, floating city above the imaginary continents of human memory. And I say to myself that it is spinning nevertheless.

IV

The Green Chamber

Each was alone now, all his knowledge of himself, his understanding, absorbed into his ears, where beats, steadily on and on and on and on, the dark red pulse.

Doris Lessing
Briefing for a Descent into Hell

Red Bank, New Jersey. 'Blood Bank,' says the facetious sannyasi, like the other facetious sannyasi in red in the red truck rolling like an open coffin towards their house. I try to laugh but I cannot summon a smile. The pain is a ball of fire in my heart, I do not have the strength to laugh, not at all.

We are driving along silently on Monmouth Drive in the bright green of this terrifying seventh of August. For the last two days, all the bottled rage of my life has been circulating through my body. Violent poison flows in my arteries, veins, little arteries, veinlets, capillaries. I have a taste of blood in my mouth and the fear of killing. It took only someone saying, '*Don't be so catlike!*' to trigger off the paranoid script and activate the dormant death machine in me. My rage is a red hyena entirely dedicated to protecting the sacred cat that is my soul. My rage ravages me and it is like a wounded animal that I drag myself to the house of the sannyasi.

First off she shows me the wheat she grows in the garage. Near the window, several shallow trays hold grass of a beautiful luminous green. She explains that it is wheat only just growing, and that she does not eat ripe wheat, only wheat like this. She grabs a handful (it really reminds me of the grass you are always tempted to eat when you are young), places it in a sort of bright metal meat grinder, and turns the handle. It produces a very dark green juice that she gathers in a plastic cup. Smiling, she hands it to me. She says that it is good, that it is pure chlorophyll. I taste it. It tastes like blood. She says yes, that, with the exception of a single atom, the atomic structure of this chlorophyll juice is similar to that of blood. That is why it is so good for one's health; it is the only thing she has eaten in the last three months. I feel nauseated.

She also shows me her room, which is green, and her closet, shimmering orange colours. She says that now the master also allows the wearing of colours derived from the colour of fire, like crimson and magenta. This is new. That up to not too long ago the sannyasi of the 'orange family' had to dress exclusively in bright orange, which is quite obvious by her closet. She laughs and shows me an Indian vest embroidered with little pieces of mirror, a silk costume that she has sewn herself, shawls and bright scarves. But this does not really interest me. I am too tired. I only ask why the colours of fire? She says that it is to remind themselves of the mission of the sannyasi through time; orange has always been the traditional colour of the Indian sannyasi.

She then leads me in the hallway, shows me where the bathroom is located, and the room of the other sannyasi. I see him through the half-opened door. He is barechested, sitting cross-legged in front of a low table. He is wearing yellow pants. I ask myself if yellow is really a colour of fire.

There is also yellow in the living room: a plush carpet. Several Huichol drawings. She tells me what they are, I would not have known. She is from Dakota, he is from Oklahoma. I ask if they have Amerindian blood. Not to their knowledge. She invites me to follow her to the veranda where I will stay for a few days.

The room is full of light. It is early afternoon. She wishes me a good stay and leaves. There is only a bed on the floor, and armchair, a candle. I sit in the armchair, a big scarlet armchair, comfortable. And I look. I look at this extraordinary room. It is a glass cage in fact, because three walls are glassed from the floor to the ceiling. Trees surround it in such a way that I feel as if I were inside a moving emerald case because, in the course of the afternoon, the sun plays through leaves, powdering and sweeping the foliage.

I remain, looking at the effect of the sun on the tree-covered walk that rustles in the breeze. There is a smell of summer, a feeling of peace. Finally. The voracious monster within calms down a bit. I do not move so as not to wake him.

Later on, around the end of the afternoon, something moving on the lawn draws my attention. I slowly rise to see what it is. It is a baby hare, all plump and bouncing on the grass. I think of Alice and the white rabbit, and my eyes follow the leveret to the edge of the wood where it dives between a fir tree and what appears to be a leprechaun. The air becomes brown. It seems much warmer. I am dropping with sleep, as the day goes down.

The hyena is also falling asleep, stretching voluptuously in my body, breathing through my mouth. I lie on the bed, my eyes half-closed. I am floating on a gold-tinged green mist, I am swinging in *La Balançoire* by Renoir, in the tears of the sun, in a vivifying cradle of greenery. And it is spinning, spinning madly above Montreal, green city, apple city, Martian City, adrift in time/space.

A carriage. The sun in the trees along the boulevard. I am Johann Wolfgang von Goethe born in Frankfurt am Main on August 28th, 1749. I am eight years old and sad because someone has just told me that I am not handsome. I am not quite sure what beauty is but I do not like it to be something I do not have. It is as if there were some human quality beyond my reach. All the same, I am sad that they are trying to depress me. I am hurt and I pray that the insensitive person who is blind to my worth will see the sacred fire that burns within me.

I have just finished the writing of *The Green Serpent*. I had a really good time and I am still marvelled at seeing the effect of words on my body and on the body of reality. I am delighted every time by their spiral aim and I am desperately trying to understand where they will lodge themselves. In what fragile, permeable, ductile part of our anatomy will they coil up, pursuing the emission of their energetic message long after our attention has wandered. I imagine writing a book in which I could have weighed each word, predicting their course, the curves they would take, the collisions they would risk, avoiding them by a hair's breadth. I imagine a book of harmony where the words cross each other, intertwine and whirl, in a disconcerting naturalness. The words wind ruby, sapphire, and topaz in the emerald fluid and form a bridge in my mental cosmos, while I live my life as if I were building a pyramid.

The *Perseo con la testa di Meduse* by Benvenuto Cellini that night was the luminous heart of a dream-like Florence in which all the dark streets converged towards him. A green brilliance emanated from the head of the Medusa, bringing her alive. She spoke to me. Said: 'Wolfgang, you are a wolf. A wolf-eros, Wolfgang.' A wolf-eros? I do not know what that is. It is one of those albino words of which you cannot determine the colour. I see the god Eros wearing a Venetian mask in some Renaissance carnival. A memory, no doubt, of a life of idleness, luxury and debauchery. As Italian as this one is German. A wolf-eros. Should I be petrified?

Christiane V. brings me the flask of blue methylene that I had requested to pursue my experiment. I am about to finalize my *Theory of Colours*, and I am meticulously studying the effect of natural and artificial colours on the soul. Blue is particularly interesting to me, insofar as I still cannot resolve its mystery. Prussian blue or blue sapphire that will spin at the heart of the prism at the Centre of the World, that will whirl and spin round and round, sunflower to the magenta magician who calls the streams of colours.

I have just heard about Marianne's marriage to Von Willemer. Outside the window, summer spreads like the multiple eyes on the peacock's feathers. The pain is all the sharper since at this moment I know for certain that the ritual distance between Marianne and me is but the repetition, the variant sorrow of a motif that our two lives have woven, and will continue to weave on the moire of memory. This adamantine love is what is truly immortal in me. It is hard nevertheless to have to endure the ravages of time in our ritual mortality.

My back is in pain. It is now cooler, a dark night. I slip under the wool blanket. Fireflies slide against the anthracite hem of my glass room. Votive fires that glow ten seconds, fade out twenty seconds, and reappear in the obscure space. Will-o'-the-wisps wake over my fever, mark my night with their ephemeral glow, constellation of membranes. While the mother magpie shudders in the reptilian vestiges of my brain, the arachnoid veers off in my memory circuits, the sounding board reverberates the echo of my cortex ringing frantically Sunday. While it is Saturday. And it is raining.

There is nobody in the house. I am cooking some rice in the kitchen, watching rain fall on Red Bank, New Jersey. 'Blood Bank.' I imagine red brooks gushing down Cooper Road, drowning stables of horses that neigh in the Red Sea, falling in torrents on the green countryside. The hyena has started stretching itself, elastic, in my belly. It is swelling, transforming itself, growing tentacles that extend through arms, grab my wrists, sink in my legs, encircle my feet. I am battling with a red octopus that clutches my throat, holds my jaws in a vice, suffocates my chest and is getting ready to vomit from my mouth. I groan, leaning against the kitchen sink in the house of the sannyasi. The rice is ready, and I should turn down the heat but I cannot move. The pain and the fear slowly consume me while a black box appears on my mental screen. I open it. I find the words: *Feel your feet and breathe deeply* written in green neon. Immediately, consciousness sinks to my feet; I feel it falling like a heavy piece of clothing around my ankles. I put out my left foot, step over the red garment of my fear and breathe in. I breathe in the red that rolls on Red Bank, like the streams of colours in the souk of dyers of North Africa. I turn down the heat. No, I shut off the burner of the electric stove. I am no longer hungry.

Taking a cushion from the living room into the glass room, I settle down to do the anger mudra. Hands joined, raised above my head, I breathe in the heavy cloud of unconsciousness that bathes my aura. I breathe out with a cry that tears the curtain of rain, while pressing my hands and my arms with all my might on the cushion. As if to strike a knife into the backs of inane bureaucrats, the papal guard of pontification and the priests of tepidness. I brandish my arms once again, breathe in all the greyness of boredom that undermines the mind. I breathe out as if to stab the word *misers* right in the heart, those petty hoarders of acknowledgment, cheap sadists of torture and mental cruelty. Soon, the rhythm lifts me, takes me above the waves of raging ego. I breathe in, breathe out; I strike out, I hit. I kill one by one the deceptive images of my shadow so that she will no longer jump in my face. It is now a dance, an energetic exorcism that fills me, empties me, that rules the fluids in my body. I collapse, exhausted. The octopus has again become a hyena in its foetal position in my belly. I feel the energy of this red mandala, spinning at a very high speed. Tears wet my face. I kneel and pick up again the rhythm of my violence. My scream swells, rises like a cloud of blood above the glass cage, invades the scarlet expanse of trees in the greenery. I tremble with fear, but the rhythm of violence is music, and I give in to this dance of death with all my body, heart, and mind. And my soul, finally, cries out for deliverance. In a long, rich, fluid cry of love that bursts everywhere, simultaneously, in the rainwater, my soul travels, and I am silent. Finally, I am silent. My soul is a flaming horse with wings of fire reflected three times in the gas pumps of a little gas station in the United States, at night, in a painting, dated 1940, by Edward Hopper. I had already seen my soul. Now, I was hearing it.

Completely spread out on the floor, my hair sticky with tears and mucus stuck to my face, I listen to the song of the rain. It resonates like an echo chamber with a crystalline lightness that makes me shiver all over and gives me the urge to laugh. In my head, my shadow has disguised itself as a black and bald warrior, with white streaked make-up. Smiling! After this massacre, that's all she can come up with!

I watch my shadow turn its back to me, moving away in the labyrinth of my subconscious, while singing softly: *'To be in/ to be in, her way/ is to be in her way.*' I open my eyes once again on the vert-de-gris fog of this rainy Saturday and decide to take a shower. My will is a Sufi dancer with green wings and a snail-shaped hat. He is spinning like a top on the mystical cone of his starched robe. It is a necromantic insect that zooms the skin of the red hyena and the scattered pieces of the octopus. I wash my hair with Herbal Essence, let the lukewarm water flow for a long time on my skin, carress my body, cleanse my memory.

It is the first of May in the year two thousand one hundred and four B.C. I am ten years old. My name is Na-Otis. I am standing in the sand. I think I am lost. Farther, there is the Sphinx. Sitting in the desert like a big cat. I feel dizzy. Several feet in front of me, to my right, there is a statue of Osiris. A golden statue. Osiris shines in the sun. It is so hot that the air wavers in front of my eyes. I am losing my balance. It must be from the heat. All of a sudden, I become the centre. The rays from the sun gather, converge on me, fall from the sky, reflect off the sand in front of me, behind me, like golden corridors. I am but an instant, a point of condensation in space that will multiply in time from one dimension to another. I have come down to live the life of Isis and I gather all the scattered members of my solar husband. Pterophorous Nephthys, my sweet sister, flies over the great pyramid. Chariots of orange fire glide above her, illuminating her.

The landscape tips over the aura of the statue of Osiris. Workers are busy building the great pyramid. I have been one of them. Memphis appears superimposed. I am a scribe in the temple of Ptah, crouched under a fig tree. I am taking a nap and I dream of penetrating the symbolic meaning of the hieroglyphs. I am Amenophis III mummified, I unroll my wrappings above the temple of Luxor up to the Nile delta. I will be Nefertari, singer of Amon, and I will write *The Book of the Dead*. I will be the young wife of an assistant archaeologist who will see the piece of turquoise silk at the bottom of Tutankhamon's tomb. It is the charming smile of Tutankhamon at the age of ten that I see drifting on the golden face of Osiris, while the sands of my conscience slide in the sandglass that flows, rain water on Red Bank, New Jersey. I get out of the shower and wrap myself in a giant mauve sponge towel.

My will is a prism that stretches towards the bottom and the top between the orange suction sun of the left hemisphere of my brain and the violet dots of my right hemisphere. My will is as deep as the forest green that surrounds me, and as acid as the apple green that poisons me. It is a slicing will that cuts and carves, reducing me to shreds while I put on warm clothes, wine-red, and I lie on the bed of my green room to read *Briefing for a Descent into Hell*, by Doris Lessing. I read this: *'There was no feeling of hostility toward the intruder in this place. On the contrary, I felt welcome there, it was as if this was a country where hostility or dislike had not yet been born.'* I understand that Doris Lessing has written this book so that I can read it here and now, in the house of the two sannyasi who have offered me this refuge in the heart of the cyclone. For hours and hours, I read, absorb this incantation in my consciousness. The words enter through my eyes, multicoloured capsules carpeting the inside of my skull, pouring lavender honey down my throat, irrigating my respiratory system, massaging my organs, running to the tip of my fingers and toes, exploding like ten thousand suns in my solar plexus. *I gotta use words when I talk to you.* Yes, yes, speak. And while she is speaking, I am listening. I can feel the wound healing up. All the insults to my intelligence, to my ability to vibrate to the universe, to my fundamental health melting in the sun of Doris Lessing's book. Speak to me, oh yes, speak to me and her soul sings from page to page and mine sings with her. It is raining nails on the sheet metal roofs of my green room, and I cry for joy in the mists of time.

I am reading in the hollow of a rainy day somewhere on Earth. Hymenopteran worker huddling in her wax cell, feeding herself off the pollen gathered by one of her sisters. Her visions are a nectar for clairvoyance and I hear the deaf sounding *om* of the hive, electric, electronic, synergetic metaphor of human labour. I am an Amazon galloping in armies of infantrymen and warriors, of tin soldiers and G.I. Joes. I am an androgyne now male, now female, two-time firefly in the black and white of the rhythm of innumerable men and women. I am an angel consumed by light, in the rustling of wings, in a heavenly population of seraphim. Laser patterns pass through me and I burn pinker and pinker. I burn all the phenylthylamin of my body in a song of love. And I hear in this instant your voices, my sisters, my brothers, from everywhere at the same time. *'And the minute fragments that compose each separate pulse beat of light (colour, sound) were one, so there were no such things as judges, but only Judge, not soldiers, but Soldier, not artists, but Artist.'* The sacred circle of unity spins like the great wheel of my mind. I am overcome by vertigo, Amazon angel, I am overcome by vertigo. Am I a speck of irony in your left eye, the keratin of your feathers, a cell of the skin of the soles of your feet? I know that my dancing is a stream that runs, from river to river, towards the ecstatic dance of the sea in your belly, Amazon angel, mother earth, father universe.

Someone knocks at the door. It is the sannyasi. She asks me if I care to join them in Bhagwan Shree Rajneesh's dynamic meditation. I don't know what it is. But I say yes. Anything to shake off this trance that takes me too high, too far, too quick and leaves me panting with vertigo, collapsed on the hard wooden floor of my green room.

The sannyasi ties a headband around my skull so the light will not reach my eyes. She explains what we are to do. We sit on the yellow plush rug in the living room. For fifteen minutes, I breathe through my mouth. More and more rapidly. It hurts my lungs. The air grows toxic but I keep at it and continue the painful *pranayama*. I hear the sannyasi panting beside me. I inhale more greedily; forge bellows breath of fire. I no longer know where I am: I hear the sannyasi swallow air, far, very far from me it seems. Has he moved? Or have I? I am completely disoriented. I cannot hear her. I no longer hear the rain either. Only the breath of fire, far, very far. And my breathing.

A gong on the tape recorder. 'For fifteen minutes, let out what comes,' says the sannyasi. She screams 'No! No! No! No!' with all her might, stomping. I crawl on the floor, I groan, I cry in the absolute darkness of this rainy afternoon in Red Bank, New Jersey. I roll my cheek on the plush rug, I rest. The sannyasin howls softly. Softly, but he is howling. For fifteen minutes. Another gong on the tape recorder. I get up again. I jump on my heels, arms lifted in the double mudra. I belch out: 'Oh, oh, oh, oh, oh, oh, oh, oh, oh.' Without stopping: 'Oh, oh, oh, oh, oh, oh, oh, oh, oh.' All the while hitting the ground with my heels to stimulate the sexual centre according to the sannyasi. I am breathless, I stop. They are bouncing, at different rhythms: 'Oh, oh, oh, oh, oh, oh, oh, oh, oh.' The floor vibrates from the thumping of heels, tickles the soles of my feet, goes up my legs, draws me, grabs me, and I start jumping again: 'Oh, oh, oh, oh, oh, oh, oh, oh, oh.' We are now bouncing in unison on the yellow plush, Sufi priests of the Aquarian age, children of America, hammering the foundations of a new world.

All of a sudden, the air is no longer the same. Lighter, rarer, *other*. I am elsewhere, here and elsewhere at the same time. The sensation flickers as soon as I try to focus on it. Air, space, here, there: everything is of another quality. So new to me that I cannot bring it to any one point of my interior cartography. I feel *suspended*: that's it: *suspended*. Or simply larger. As if I had, suddenly, grown and was now breathing air that I had never breathed before. To have your head in the clouds. That must be what it is like to have your head in the clouds. A cool wind, to my left, I am blindfolded, my head turned straight to the front, and yet I can see, behind my left ear, through my left ear, it seems, an ethereal blue form brushing against me. Something not of this world brushing against me. Is it you, Ariel, my soul and Holy Ghost? Is it you, Amazon angel? Who is it?

In a few seconds, the sensation vanishes. And, as the French say, an angel flies by. I start bouncing again. 'Oh, oh, oh, oh, oh, oh, oh, oh, oh.' A third gong. To be still. To feel the moving centre, volume, blue globe between my hands that moves infinitely slow, quartz and mica, polished on the sandpaper of time. I follow in softness the energetic currents that cut across my body, I can balance them with precision. The sweat forms at my forehead, soaking the headband, smothering me. The tape seems finished, there is no more music. I hear silence. I tear off the headband, wipe my face. The sannyasi have disappeared. It is still raining. I return to my glass cage that has begun to sink in darkness. My belly hurts. My menstruation has started. I am bleeding abundantly.

I spend the late afternoon spread out, a bit feverish, going back and forth through the boundary between the two worlds. It is red behind my eyes, it is red in me, and it flows from me a red torrent. Young red woman, forevermore beautiful, I empty myself of my blood. I flow from the source, for I am from the fire and the abyss, I am from the ankh, red rose tornado, Amazon angel androgyne, builder of cathedrals in the sky. I am transformed, night and mist, in the crematory oven of my uterus. And, while the archangel Raphael starts playing the piano, I surf ecstatically on the bloody waves of my Pacific belly. The clear notes spurt out through the open window of the sannyasi's room, creep between the glass laths of the veranda, roll into the room, like foam, wrap me in the suave halo that rocks and consoles me, heals me. I sink, blood and tears of ecstasy, in the black bath of the coming night, heavy cape, on Red Bank, New Jersey.

The rising sun wakes me. It is a beautiful day. The yellow star navigates between green waves of foliage and I laze about, stretch out, breathe. My will is a dancing dervish who sings: *'All I ask of you/ is forever/ to remember me/ as loving you/ Abdul Allah/ Simbdel Allah/ Abdul Allah/ Simbdel Allah.'* A cicada sings, shrilly, in the rising heat. It smells good: the earth, the chlorophyll, the summer. I notice, at the edge of the woods, there where the little hare had fled the day before yesterday, a leprechaun. The same one. Green hat, Irish beard. A tiny St. Patrick of shadows and leaves, of sun games and imagination. It is going much better, thank you. But why did he have to enter, Prince of Cups, straight into my life? So that today at last, in the midst of the bath of greenery, I can say: 'It's going much better, thank you. I remember.'

Why did he have to enter, Prince of Wands, into the dark room of my memory? To open the door to the fire? Why did she have to enter, Princess of Swords, in the mined fields of my violence? So that I will bow down, at last? Why did they have to enter, Prince and Princess of Pentacles, Amazon angel androgyne, galloping on a magical black horse? So that I will rise up at last, so that I will look around me, at the trees? The sun in the trees. A green serpent of light suspended in the radiant green of trees.

I open the door slowly. The sannyasi is standing there, fist raised to my level: 'I was going to knock.' He smiles. He says that the sannyasi has gone to work. To earn a living, she does go-go dancing on Sunday, at the Dolphin in Long Beach. He asks me how I am. I am unable to answer. I smile. I try to say something but nothing comes out. I am sad. He notices. He says that anger comes from birth. One must learn to breathe well. He smells of tiger balm. He hugs me. His warmth is comforting. He kisses me on the forehead. I step outside.

It is warm. I walk in the meadow of Woodland Farm. I stride over fences, jump, run, turn a somersault, I spin like a top. Then I stop. The grass is a dream-like green. I am wearing a lilac dress. I look at the colour of my dress, for everything moves and trembles, I have arrived in the space of a dream from twelve or thirteen years ago. A gigantic lilac statue is crumbling, pulverizing itself in white powder in the green English landscape. I am not a statue. I am moving lilac that stirs and shivers with the north wind. I await the wild snow of combustion but I do not explode. It snows abundantly in my head, the borderline between reality and fiction becomes blurred, melts in a beautiful August afternoon on the sunlit meadow of Woodland

Farm. I start running again to the swimming pool, at the other end of the field. No one. I undress and I slip in, naked, into the turquoise water that engulfs me in coolness. Sunflowers are growing high along the wire fence, displaying their yellow faces on the pure blue summer sky of Red Bank, New Jersey. I swim underwater, in the aquatic silence, bathyscaphe, happy as sand.

My will is a green star dancing around the fire, our grandfather fire, Atlantean memory consuming the mould, whistling and whirling around the magical mauve fire. My will is a green star with six branches that glitter on the backdrop of polyglot words, hieroglyphs, cuneiforms, numbers, the Morse Code, Chinese characters, Arabic script, and the language of the heart. My will is a green star that shines above the ruins of Babel. It burns, nevertheless, in my solar plexus.

During the American Airlines flight 333 between Chicago and Montreal I hear the haunting tune of that little girl I met long ago in the Mayan ruins of Chichen Itza. She sang, all day long, without stopping 'San Miguel, San Miguel, San Miguel' in her monotone, fragile and, paradoxically, passionate little voice.

I burst into the mass of oxygen, nitrogen, argon and other rare gases suspended above the swimming pool. How good it is, air. *Prana*. I am clutching to the bars of the ladder to come out of the water and find myself face to face with the great blue goddess. She is standing in a violet flame spread out like a fan behind her indigo hair that lights the wall of rock along the swimming pool. I did not know that the sannyasi has finished the fresco she had undertaken at the beginning of the summer. Yesterday's flood has faded the colours, has drowned the red wings of the blue extraterrestrial that flies above the waves hemmed by a navy blue sea above which dally three dolphins whose bodies bend in a circular arc. To the right, a being more or less human, blue, and fitted with a pair of red-flame wings, flies over a virgin forest, of dark green dulled by rainwater. Through the luxurious vegetation, a pink serpent unfolds itself and then coils under a blurred being, half-human, half-animal, also red and blue. Finally, a foetal form with an indigo body surrounded by red flames seems to shoot up from a bright fire covering the height of the wall. Inside the lips of fire, a hem of violet flames that turns dark blue and, finally, the white light. I stay there standing, in front of the fire drawn on the wall. It reminds me of something.

Uncle François holds me in his arms above a wooden stove and Mother says that I am no longer a baby, that I will soon be one year old, that I will throw away my pacifier by myself like a big girl. I feel the warm breath of the fire on my face and I suck on my pacifier, then I open my mouth and I let it fall in the fire. There is blue, mauve, in the red of the fire and it reminds me of something.

He throws me in the fire! He throws me in the fire! Auschwitz, 1944. Cremation of Celia Rosenberg. She is burning. It is not me. I am a baby. I am a big girl now. I am throwing my pacifier in the fire.

He throws me in the fire! He throws me in the fire! Arles, 1349. The Inquisition is burning a young Moorish woman of seventeen for witchcraft and dealings with the Devil. She is dancing in the fire. I see her dancing. It is not me. I am a baby. I am a big girl now. I throw my pacifier in the fire.

He throws me in the fire! He throws me in the fire! Chichen Itza, 1192. The sacrifice of a baby eleven months old that is thrown down into the inferno lit at the bottom of the dry *cenote* so that Chac-Mool, God of Rain, will make water fall from the sky. I am burning. I see the flames around me. It is me. It is not me. I am a baby. I am a big girl now. I throw my pacifier in the fire.

There is blue, mauve, in the red of the fire. It reminds me of something. The fire typhoon of Lemuria. The flaming spirals through which one has to levitate to avoid being swallowed by glaucous monsters wallowing in the Green Sea. I am turning, twirling, I am wheeling between the wheels of fire. My nervous system is sizzling. Under my transparent skin, the adrenalin irrigates my body, branching, growing according to a spiral system that catapults me, interstellar dust in the silver hair of the nearest spiral nebula.

It reminds me of something. Yes, but now, what? What? A kryptonite pyramid stealing my strength, sucking away my courage, syphoning my faith. But it is not solid. It is but a structure of green waves that I can sweep away with a glance, drive to the very bottom of the cosmos. Because I want to see the fire. The blue, the mauve, in the red of the fire. To feel its breath on my face.

Oh it is you my soul, my love, archangel Michael. I recognize the rhythm of your breathing, the smell of your breath, the taste of your aura. I open my eyes on the black fire burning in your eyes. I throw myself in the fire of your eyes, my soul, my love, Miguel, at the other end of the world. 'San Miguel, San Miguel, San Miguel,' sings the little red girl that haunts my memory. San Miguel, Miguel. I read in the eyes of fate and of flames. I love you, Miguel, and I remember the heat of your breath on my forehead. The crystal lozenge that gives me access to other worlds. That is the source of the violet flame that licks me, lifts you, Miguel, takes us, irresistible mauve fire from the Tierra del Fuego to the Andean Cordillera, from Amazonia and Central America to the Sierra Madre and to the Rockies, runs like a brush fire through the Prairies, surging into James Bay, and flows, lava of ruby and amethyst, on the Abitibi, the Témiscamingue, Lac Saint-Jean, engorges the Saguenean Fjords a moment before sweeping the whole Saint-Laurent Valley, penetrating the streets of Montreal, mauve watercolour water where I sleep in the hollow of a spider's web that shines, magenta, in the sleep of an Amazon angel, androgyne.

V

Melemele Aloha Au Ia'oe

Andjela, my cat, I understood! This is it, this is enlightenment! I have reached samadhi, nirvana, satori, paradise! The veil tears open, and I am bedazzled! The catamaran pitches on the cerulean blue of Honolulu Bay, I dance the hula to the sound of a Hawaiian band playing *Guantanamera*, while the light-boat slides on the black water between Yelapa and Puerto Vallarta.

The setting sun gleams on the dance floor of the Aikane-Honolulu. Everyone follows the roll, holding glasses of Blue Hawaii in hand. Mauka, towards the Koolau Mountains, Honolulu cuts its skyscrapers on the drizzle iridescent with rainbows. I recognize the Diamond Head from Hawaii 5-0, but I understood, Andjela, I understood.

This boat is but a variant of the invariant *boat*. I am cruising in the warm waters of the Pacific, as I navigated long ago in the cold seas of the Antarctic. I close my eyes on seaspray wetting my face. I am a biocomputer adrift in the mists of time. A white liner majestically splits the blue Mediterranean waters. I am sailing on a nave, skating on the sand in front of Hong Kong at night. There are strong winds on the ferry between Oka and Rigaud. 'You must not climb on the gangway,' says Father. I am standing in a felucca; I am nauseated. An Egyptian scribe is kneeling on the floor of the small boat, his arms joined together around my knees. The canoe hisses on the sombre waters of Lake Wapizagong. A plane breaks the sound barrier, and granite blocks crumble. An animatronic crocodile's teeth are clattering near the pirogue cutting across the Disney jungle. I smile in the foreground of Amsterdam as it passes through the purring movie camera. The *bateau mouche* moves rapidly between two rows of decorated barges. The gondolier interrupts his *'Funiculi, funicula'*, shows a house eaten up by *vert-de-gris*, says that it was Goethe's house in Venice. He tells me to hold the jib, that we could capsize. The sailboat veers out at full speed between glaciers reflecting in the lake. I scream that I don't know what it is. I am afraid of falling in the icy waters. I am walking head down in a grey iron submarine. Santorini shines bright, Atlantean, in the first glimmers of dawn; fades away until it becomes but a minute white point in my gaze riveted on the horizon, while the boat takes me towards Crete.

I am eighteen years old, feverish. For ten days, I have had a fever. I do not do anything. I look at the ceiling. There is nothing. It is a wooden ceiling, plain. When I wake in the morning, right away I look above me, to my left, to see if the head of the sailor is still there. And, every morning, it is there. It is a bearded man of about forty. A man from the sixteenth century. A Dutch sailor. I do not know how come I know he's a sailor, a Dutchman, from the sixteenth century. But it does not matter. It is because I am sick, because of the fever. I feel good. I look at the sailor, on the ceiling. It is weird that I should have the impression he is dressed in blue because the ceiling is just brown, after all. He was born in Delft. It is when I read the word *Delft* in my book that I started to see him. I am reading *Remembrance of Things Past*, by Marcel Proust, and I am telling the story as I go along to my little brother who says that I am going crazy. I say no, that it is because of the little yellow wall in the painting by Vermeer that Bergotte dies when he goes to look at it one last time. My little brother says that he does not know who Vermeer or Bergotte are, that he prefers Bobino. I look at the sailor on the ceiling: he seems to be smiling. He understands. I fall asleep and dream that I am sailing on the ocean, the open sea of the Azores. The swelling is strong but I hold the bar firmly, my eyes squinting in the wind.

The band has stopped playing. On a drum roll, a young dancer from the Samoan Islands jumps up on the dance floor. He is holding a burning torch in each hand. Drum roll. We form a circle around him. He is juggling the torches, throws them, catches them with disconcerting agility. While he is swaggering in a dance of fire that takes your breath away, I bathe my face in the last golden rays of the sun.

You are speaking, shaman, my sister. You are drawing circles with your hands. You are laughing, cursing. Words rush out of your mouth, live insects, crackling like golden moths around you and nestling themselves in the blanks of my map of reality. You say 'body'. And I see. You say 'heart'. And I see. You say 'mind'. And I see. You say that the body, the heart and the mind functioning in synergy are the soul. *'Soul. As a kid I used to think people were coming from the "souls" of their feet.'* You say 'spirit', shaman, my sister. And I see. You are speaking and your speech bathes me, shaman, my sister. I watch you speaking. I let your voice caress the pink pavilions of my ears, resonate on my eardrums and my mind lets go. You are soothing my mind, shaman, my sister. Your word is a balm for my mind.

At the beginning, I had about ten thousand articles of faith. My little brother took them away from me. I only had five thousand left. My love took them from me. Then I had only one thousand. The archangel Gabriel took them from me. I only had five hundred left. My sister took them from me. Only one hundred articles of faith were left. And you are now taking them from me, shaman, my sister. Will you leave me some, or will I have to live like a warrior?

The dancer is still turning, rolling fire in front of my half-opened lids. I spread out the field of my consciousness into my ethereal body. I must resemble these mutants with prominent foreheads and reptilian heads topped by the golden crest I often draw. I then rise slowly above the catamaran. The Samoan dancer, seen from above, resembles Shiva, who would have descended on earth for a cruise in the setting sun. I fly for some time above the Pacific, just to admire the scenery. I go as far as Bali, arriving just in time to see the sun collapse in a mass of ochre clouds. From there, I teletransport myself on the Thursday of Jupiter, pink planet where a scientific congress of the ten thousand galaxies is being held. I slip incognito into the crowd, hidden behind my heart-shaped sunglasses. I painfully manage to reach my laboratory. The crowd is thick and very animated in the spiral streets of Thursday. Everyone is talking about the alignment of the planets for October 1982, and many say that that is much too early. Some astronomers produce holographic demonstrations of the alignment on the Main Square. Some mathematicians exchange their equations through ultrasounds, a neurologist projects a passable visualization of Maitreya above the translucid dome.

I set my attention on the password *sol*, which electrically activates the opening of the door, controlled by an ultra-sensitive receiver with mental imprints. Pollyanna greets me with a vibrant: *'Isn't it a nice day to ride our bicycle, sister?'* I say yes, sure, but I have other things to do. She is saddened by this, but quickly regains her optimism, saying that, after all, I am the boss. She brings me a large glass of milk. I say that I would much prefer a cognac. She says, no way. She watches over my health, as if it were the apple of her eye. I say to myself, well good, after all, it is true. She is right. That is no reason to drink milk. I ask her to bring me a Coke. She grumbles, but still goes towards the kitchenette, bringing back my glass of milk.

I take advantage of her absence to call Albert Einstein and Sonia Delaunay. Before I can say 'rabbit', they materialize in my laboratory. Einstein wears an old mauve sweater, green pants and yellow leather shoes. He offers me his hand. I beckon him to sit in the white leather lazyboy chair handed down by my great-grandfather. Sonia is wearing a red dress streaked with blue, orange earrings, blue shoes and indigo eye shadow. She gives me a loud kiss on each cheek. She smells of soap, and it dizzies me somewhat. Graciously, she greets Mr. Einstein, who rises immediately and folds in an elegant bow. She says, all pink with confusion: 'Please, please.' I beckon her to sit in the black silk love seat handed down by my great-grandmother. She complies. Pollyanna returns with my Coke. She asks what my guests would wish to drink. Einstein would gladly have a root beer, Mrs. Delaunay would not say no to a strawberry drink.

Pollyanna trots along, all smiles, towards the kitchen. I sit on the black-and-white checkered stool handed down by the Amazon angel herself. An angel passes. Pollyanna breezes in with the drinks and slips out to let us work.

I run a nervous hand over my golden crest and say to myself, well now, how shall

I put my problem to them? They are both staring at me with their candid blue look. I talk about Gurdjieff, Ouspensky, Mrs. Blavatsky, Oscar Ichazo, John Lilly. They nod. I tell them that I would like to make a list of the different states of consciousness through my memory. They consult one another in low voices.

After five minutes of confabulation, Sonia beckons me to lie down on the yellow sofa handed down from you, Andjela. Sonia Delaunay places her cool hands on my forehead; Albert Einstein softly massages the soles of my feet. Their minds meet above me; multicoloured laser rays gather in a prism of light into which I fall headfirst.

I am at the bottom of a well. I can hardly breathe. The right side of my body feels like it is paralyzed. It feels like pins and needles. As soon as I close my eyes, I see sand. I am walking in the sand at La Jolla in California. But I am not in La Jolla, California. I am in my room. All the Pharaohs of Egypt are pushing at the doors of my consciousness to get in, all the Maya-Toltec gods, all the extraterrestrials. Mercy! I will never again take a single line of cocaine I swear, but leave me alone, leave me alone! I am crawling on an iron gangplank above the abyss. Lucifer is coming forward on the gangplank. He is wearing a pastel jacket, a peach-coloured shirt, and smiles broadly. He approaches, sarcastic, tells me: 'So, we've finally hit bottom?' That is when I straighten up in a formidable bound and deal him a karate blow in the solar plexus. *Vade retro Satana*! He grabs me by the hair, but I scratch his face. I strike his nose and he starts to bleed. He lets me go, then leaves. I cry, my hands bloodied, my nose glued to the cold metal of the gangplank under which flows a river of blood. The next day, I notice that the blood has splashed the silk of my pink screen. Dejected, I wash it with clear water, then javel water. I draw the face of Ariel on the screen, in watercolours. Ariel, my soul, the Holy Ghost.

Slowly, I emerge from the third hell. I hold my breath. My back is pressed against the wall of a house under construction, in Puerto Vallarta, at nighttime. I am sure he wants to kill me. I have run away, through street after street. I have climbed up to here. Someone from the house is coming. How come this place is occupied, if the house is still under construction? The man has turned on the light. He is wearing pyjamas. He says: '*Que se pasa aqui?*' I remain hidden in the shadow. I hear the steps in the street coming closer. I do not know where to go. I stop breathing. Then, he says my name. And, hearing him speak my name, I dissipate the second hell and jump with both feet in the street, beside him. I say I thought he was going to kill me. He laughs. We are walking by the sea. It is a full moon. The Pacific rolls its violent waves. We are walking on the low wall that looks onto the beach some fifteen feet below. At a certain moment, it becomes narrower and he courteously beckons me to pass in front of him. I freeze. I say no thank you, that I am afraid he will throw me down into the raging ocean. He laughs, says: *'Pero usted no tambien!'* – and passes in front of me. I follow him slowly, trying to remove myself from the second hell.

I am unable to do anything. It is grey outside. I feel sick, feel like crying, I am trembling, and do not remember what I said, what I did, where I was, or with whom. I drank too much. I cannot take anymore of this. I have a vision of a black wolf with pointed ears. Grey rays come out of his eyes, forming a wire mesh that crisscrosses his face. In his head, a small red-eyed wolf glows grey and makes a double transfer. I am afraid of dying. I call the archangel Michael. He tells me to breathe, to go for a walk. I walk, breathing in deeply, to dissipate the wolf from Hell number one glued to the back of my head. I breathe in, breathe out, in and out, until it becomes completely unstuck and vanishes in an alcoholic steam.

I should really give up smoking. I am on my third pack of tobacco today. I have a hard time breathing. I am nauseated, have no energy, no will to move. I light another last cigarette before starting to do what I have to do. I will never be able to stop smoking. Too bad! It is eleven-thirty. I have half a pack of cigarettes left. I am writing an article entitled: 'How I stopped smoking while writing this text, as in the *Reader's Digest.*' I am not writing. I am contemplating each word, one by one, in the blue halo of cigarette smoke. Good. I have had enough. I am going to smoke them all and, at midnight, it will be over. I chain-smoke. I am anxious to stop. I am feeling more and more sick to my stomach, more and more anxious to stop smoking. I no longer finish them. I put them out when they are three-quarters burnt, half-burnt, quarter-burnt. Five to midnight and I have five cigarettes left. I light them all, one after the other, slip them between my lips. And I go take a look at myself in the bathroom mirror. I suck in, I suck in. My eyes sting, my heart is pounding. I know these are my last ones. One to midnight, I am checking the time. At midnight exactly, I put out the last five cigarettes of my life, one after the other. Oof! I feel atrociously sick. I throw up. I feel dirty, poisoned. I take a warm shower, then cold, it ejects me from limbo.

Archangel Gabrielle says: '*Feel your feet. Don't forget to feel your feet.*' I move my head, my neck, my shoulders, my elbows, my wrists to the rhythm of the drum that emphasizes the time that flows, solid and undulating. I do a rotation with my rib cage, my pelvis, my hips move in staccato with the drumbeats. I lift my knees, my feet, light and lyrical on the hard wood surface. I shake my whole body in a happy chaos, violent, ecstatic. I stand still to hear the gong of silence in my heart. It is autumn in the Eastern Townships. I put a woolen jacket over my sweat-soaked clothing and walk in the flamboyant gold of autumn. I am walking on the ground. There are even some geese waddling near the pond. It feels good to be alive, on the earth. It has been such a long time.

We are walking through the hall. It is the porpoise dance. We are fifty in the Arican chapel at Maui. Sixty travel in space to the rhythm of the drum and cymbals. I step forward, back up, change directions. I spiral, walk diagonally. The others pass in front of me, around me, beside me. No one collides with me. No one stops me. I go where I am going, and I am going in the rhythm that beats under my feet. I follow the path of my feet, where my heart takes me. I do not have to settle on an itinerary. I surrender to the movement inside me. I spiral in the tangles of the courses, in the traffic of souls under the empire of the spirit that floats, mauve, above this living organism, our porpoise dance in the first heaven.

The archangel Raphael knocks me down on the sand, shouting. I fight back, in fun, and then stop. I give up. He is holding my wrists in his hands. He holds tight, then sees that I am surrendering. His eyes lose themselves in my eyes. *In the mirror of thee, I see me.* We both close our eyes in vertigo at the same time. He squeezes against me, I shiver under the caress of his hairy chest and flamboyant erection. I am in seventh heaven.

In my heart's lotus, a little blue Buddha trembles on his throne of light supported by four white translucent horses. I sit on a lotus leaf in his heart on a meditation cushion, somewhere on earth. It is five-fifteen in the morning. From my heart springs a blue ray which transmutes me into Buddha. Beams of red and yellow energy radiate from my body, spread out over the earth, flooding it with yellow-red consciousness awakening energy; I am a blue sparkle in the vast body of Buddha pulsing the mantra of the mental body of earth. It is the heaven of ten thousand suns.

The sky falls on my head, a pillar of white light. The stars turn between pyramids and I burn, sun between sun, propelled to the speed of light, a universe expanding at the speed of light. I burn love in the heart of Love, Milky Way of the nebular Amazon angel.

Sonia Delaunay passes her hand in front of my eyes, saying: 'The goddess is waking now. The goddess is waking.' I return her smile. Einstein passes his fingers through his white mane, stretching, rising to the starry skies. The laboratory has disappeared. We are flying in space, Sonia Delaunay, Einstein and I, and all the scintillating lights, planetary ellipses, configurations of constellations. All this strangely resembles a giant computer. '*The human mind is the computer of the universe*,' says Einstein. While I tumble down towards Polaris, I try to concentrate on the Great Bear to transfer gamma towards the Constellation of the Swan. It does not work. The stars are dancing. The whole sky is dancing, but I have lost track and can no longer even find the Great Bear. '*I didn't say "your" mind,*' specifies Einstein smiling indulgently at me. *'I said "the" human mind.'* *'Yours, Sonia's, mine and every human mind since the beginning of Time.'* Having said this, Einstein tumbles backward and disappears in a black hole, gently waving to me. Sonia Delaunay starts getting more and more luminous, she ends up exploding in a white quasar on the interstellar backdrop.

Soon, I am sailing above Montreal, orange city asleep in the hollow of mandarin dreams, city of the sleeping, golden angel, goldilocks and pumpkin, in the gleaming membranes of the intellectual archangel.

The dance of fire ends in a salvo of applause. I am still numb from sleep when the young dancer approaches me, smiles at me, makes a strange gesture, delicate, with his right hand, a sort of secret mudra that I do not know. He says, *'Melemele aloha au ia'oe.'* I am dumbfounded. He disappears to the rear of the boat. What does '*Melemele aloha au ia'oe*' mean? The young Hawaiian guide smiles, touches the bright yellow fabric of my sun dress, and says: *'Yellow, I love you.'* It means: *'Yellow, I love you.'*

Standing in front of *The Ambassadors* by Holbein, at the National Gallery, Hubert Aquin, encircled with a golden halo like a saint in Piero Della Francesca, is reading the museum card which explains the anamorphous process used by Holbein in his painting. He steps back, comes slightly forward to the left, up to the moment when he sees the cuttlefish bone transform itself into a skull. He then puts on his bowler hat, takes his umbrella, and goes out for a walk in the London fog to meet our dearest Bobby Watson, with whom he has an appointment, is that not so, dear Miguel?

In the plane between Los Angeles and Chicago, I fall asleep, Andjela.

VI

In the Heart of Rose

The road between Haena and Lumahai Beach borders the Pacific, zigzags through the odours of eucalyptus bathing this Sunday morning where I have been walking cheerfully for hours. When I arrive at the beach, where *South Pacific* was filmed, it must be around noon. It is completely deserted. After searching for a half-hour, I find the path that goes down to the beach under a cover of banyan trees. The sand spreads in a half-moon before me. Petrified lava has formed black reefs, against which pounds the peacock sea.

I climb on one of them. Sheets of lukewarm water filled with small black fish and fragile crabs that sparkle in the crevices. It is hot. I take off my shrimp-coloured skirt and the broad salmon-coloured blouse. I keep my bikini on since I hear the first Sunday picnickers call out to one another under the trees. I had planned to stop here just a few moments and swim at Hanalei Bay, but this water is so tempting! It draws me like a magnet. I dive into the magnetic blue.

I am rolling in erotic rumours of the Pacific. I spread out, starfish, in the ebb and flow. I Estelle, I Valentine, I Iris, I Angel, my lovely Yvelle, in the indigo bath of my heart.

A dolphin smiles at me from the bottom of the sea. I climb like an amazon on his grey-blue back. He dashes out towards the depths of the Pacific, dives in a tailspin into the abyss. I make bubbles, delighted to have finally learnt to breathe under water. A channel of warm water carries us to Easter Island. Gathering speed, the dolphin heads for the south, bypasses the Tierra del Fuego, soars towards the Sargasso Sea. Eels cling to my hair, my arms, wrap themselves around my ankles, my legs. I scream in horror, desperately clinging to the neck of a dolphin who cuts through the heavy and grey saline waters of the Atlantic. We cross the multi-dimensional electronic barrier of the Bermuda Triangle. The water progressively takes on a pink colour as we approach the illuminated city of Atlantis.

A horde of armed knights guards the entrance. They draw up their halberds and grunt dully behind iron masks. Their armour sparkles, black, in front of the white megalopolis. I finally rid myself of the last eel writhing around my neck. I stand on the back of the dolphin. I stare directly at the warrior with eyes that shine hot bricks behind his iron mask. I say: 'I am Laïka, pink star of the ten thousand suns. I have the right to enter here.' Immediately, the knights push back to the left and right, opening a passage. A pack of bloody monsters appear suddenly in front of us. The dolphin pulverizes them with sonar hits. From their remains rise vampire bats fluttering their wings, blinding me, forming a nasty whirlpool under the belly of the dolphin, getting ready to tear us to pieces. The dolphin starts scrambling their radar by emitting ultrasounds. I drive them away by crossing my hands in front of my face as in the invulnerability mudra, palm turned towards my aggressors. White-skinned, blond-haired Atlanteans come towards me. Others with red skin and black hair already hold my hands, warming them in their hot palms transmitting their message of welcome. A group of young girls with skin black as the deep of night dance in a circle around me, a sort of aquatic ballet that throws the dolphin in an apparent state of absolute ecstasy. I finally join the yellow-skinned, slanted-eyed Atlanteans who guide me in silence through the dry-iced passage of Atlantis, up to the amphitheatre where galactic-desert blue men and women are gathered.

One of them quickly comes towards me, smiling. She is a shaman, three times extraterrestrial incarnated this time in the United States to create unity rituals. I recognize her. For many years, she has guided me in the streets of the cities of my dreams. She hugs me, holds me close to her heart, and says: '*I fall back thousands of years into our future.*'

She then takes me off to a screening room. Do you know what I see appearing around me, *ma belle* Yvelle? Four times with a toothy smile in front of the temple of sacred writing in Chichen Itza, you appear in that dated photograph. She tells me to wait for her, that she will return. I sit on the floor in the centre of the room and look at you smiling at me, Yvelle, *ma belle*.

I examine you with such intensity that you end up becoming animated, phantom of light, miming the subtle balance of a tightrope walker. I find you terrified to death in the heart of your fear's red cyclone. You listen to the beating of its heart opening in a rainbow bowing to earth, and find yourself turning at the centre, spacewoman, through time.

I catch you storming against the blinding lightning that streaks your territory. You listen to the orange pulse of lightning transmuted in tongues of fire and lasers of kryptonite.

I catch you drowning in tears, sinking in your sadness. You listen to its breath, and Venus shines in the night sky of your soul.

I am suffused with memories of stardust, Yvelle. Cosmic raindrops fall on my head, galactic snowflakes, moon drops, sun flakes, Venusian dust fall on me like a pink blessing. I hear your heart beating, pink, all around me and your spirit that breathes, mauve, in the stellar winds.

The blue shaman returns, shuts off the electricity. Then you disappear, *belle* Yvelle, in front of the temple of sacred writings. The shaman has seated herself in front of me, in the dark. She asks me in a low voice to take the position of the humility mudra, hands joined and head lowered.

She then starts singing the universal mantra in a surprisingly deep voice. I join her in her prayer and descend slowly from beta to alpha. My cerebral waves go from forty cycles per second to fourteen cycles per second. I count down, starting from one hundred, while going down a rope ladder oscillating in the void of my larynx. The sound arises from my belly, in the echo chamber of my *corps de gloire*, a fountain gushing from my chest and throat, tickling my lips, my nose, my third eye, the top of my head, my nape. It rolls in my skull and comes out of my mouth like the outflow of milk that coats me in sugar.

The shaman starts transmitting thought forms that imprint directly in my brain. At the beginning, I do not quite know how to receive these moving diagrams that I do not understand, and I feel my mind cramping under the task. She senses my panic because the rhythm of the transmission slows down. I receive the image of an entanglement of live vegetable wires. It is impossible to untangle, it gives me a headache. Then I clearly hear the words: *'I gotta use words when I talk to you.'* She laughs, then says: *'What about, even better, a written translation?'* And, on the cathode screen of the right hemisphere of my brain, I can see the words form: *'Tengo hablar con palabras cuando yo hablo con usted.'* Right after, I hear her: *'Please excuse my broken Spanish. Do you feel better now?'* I think, yes, but I also think that I would like it better if she translated into French and I wonder if she has understood. It is then that the tangle grey of plant-like wires clears up and starts making sense. I recognize a bizarre head from a painting by Max Ernst, copied in a few seconds from a surrealist art book several years ago. I am struck by the rigorous precision of the sketch, because I pay no attention and content myself with jotting down several traits without taking my eyes off of the original. I am in a hurry and want to typify graphically this beautiful grey head which looks like card-board and spider webs to make up a mask. Right then, it appears to me, very life-like, on a piece of rough paper.

I understand that the shaman is just sending thought forms that are in sort of dotted lines I have to fill out with my own memory.

Coming out of the grey head, a scroll, which spreads itself above her, has written on it: *The Seven Laws of Mercury*. I am a bit disappointed. I thought myself advanced enough in my studies to pass directly to the three laws of the sun. I think I hear resonating among the vibrations of the universal mantra the words: '*Not yet, not yet.*'

The head of the woman of a hundred heads – for it must surely be her – disappears, and I see once again the cathodic screen. I read this: *First law of Mercury: All is Spirit, Spirit is All.* A crowned, grey serpent springs from the left, another identical one from the right. They cross and wrap themselves around three nails driven into the gloom of a solar eclipse. Between their heads mutually hypnotized, forms a drop of mercury. It is the first card of the Dakini tantric Tarot, Mercury.

The card grows dim, vanishes little by little, disappears into the eclipse. I see my hand tracing the name of the shaman when she did not exist for me. To write her name provoked her existence, I have thus called her, so that one day we would be reunited here to decipher together the laws of Mercury. I hear her voice rising in the dark room. She says that Yvelle Swanson is coming. It is then that I ask myself what she sees. I see her then watching the vision of what we are doing now, in fifty copies, in synergy. I wonder if I could have perceived her if she had not already related her vision of Big Sur.

The dance of mental porpoises calms down and the words illuminate the screen: *Second Law of Mercury: What is above is the same as what is below.* A green lizard slides its little, stinging, pointed head between an apple falling from the sky, tail down, and another rising to the sky, tail up. The two apple tails find themselves opposite one another and the little lizard seems to want to bring them together with its tongue. It is the fifty-seventh card of the Dakini: the card of Temptation.

I see the card in my left hand and *The Divine Comedy* in my right hand. I am reading a passage out loud to my best friend:

> *Whence she, who saw me, clearly as myself,*
> *To calm my troubled mind, before I ask'd*
> *Open'd her lips, and gracious thus began:*
> *With false imagination thou thyself*
> *Makest dull, so that thou seest not the thing,*
> *Which thou hadst seen, had that been shaken off.*[*]

I am asking my best friend if he cannot see at what point the evident analogical sense of the excerpt of the first song of *Paradise* is a brilliant demonstration of the pitfalls of analogical thought. He answers that he really does not understand my mystical trip, seeing that I am the most vulgar materialist he knows. My arms drop. I am not even offended, which is not like me. And I say to him: 'But it is the same thing, evidently!'

The image becomes blurred. The shaman whispers: *'Don't let the ego take over. Slay the ego. Surrender to your essence.'* The image clears up, I can once again see the screen. And the words: *Third Law of Mercury: All is vibration.* A sort of stylized

---
[*]Translated by Henry F. Cary.

Buddha appears on a snowy Tibetan backdrop. His hat stretches out until it merges into a curtain that rises in the landscape. Above his forehead, in what is the first level of his hat, shines a drop-shaped ruby. A second drop-shaped ruby hides his nose and mouth. It falls in the heart of the ruby set down slantwise on a bed of pink flowers that seems to be growing, there, in the snow. In the heart of the heart of the ruby, a little rose quartz heart. And, in the background, the blue of a river. It is card forty-four of the Dakini, that of the Drop of the Heart.

François says that he will remain in telepathic contact. I tell myself it is true that he is crazy. For one week there is a vibration in the middle of my forehead, all day, all night, like something unwinding. Nonstop. That week everyone was called François because it is the *franc soi** and, at that level, we are all the same person. It is not long after that that I feel them pass over Montreal, indigo city trembling in the wind, ultramarine seascape in the heart of the cosmic archangel. The whole house is trembling, and I am trembling also. It is a shudder of marvel, of excitement, of joy, I do not know. It feels good to feel the uni-

---
*Franc: loyal, true, frank; *soi*: self.

verse pulsate on your skin, in your heart, in your brain. They say they wish an exchange of information, and I say: 'All right.' I say: 'OK, OK.' But I am wondering what they want to know.

The shaman raises the tone of her voice in my head: *'Don't get attached to your mission. Just do it'*. The fourth Law of Mercury, then, appears: *All is double.* A bright yellow bolt of lightning splits the space of the screen at the centre. At the foreground, a cobra lifts its large head. On it, drawn directly on the scales, the hieroglyph of the double. It is the thirty-ninth card of the Dakini, that of the Power of the Serpent.

I am sitting in another dark room, in another time, in front of another blue shaman. The double of herself, with her name. Her double in the heart of rose.

On the cathodic screen, the Fifth Law of Mercury is now spelled out: *What goes up must come down.* An atomic mushroom takes form on the screen, red and yellow. It comes from a hash pipe that we can only guess at faintly in a mass of black clouds. The mushroom collides with a first stratum of red clouds, pierces and pushes with even more force on the next stratum that it lifts but still does not succeed in piercing. Two other red cloud strata separate the atomic explosion from the convolutions of a human brain that sets down above, as on a platter. It is the fortieth card of the Dakini, that of Consciousness Expansion.

My conscience flies like a phoenix in the blue sky. I fly and burn and fly, arms stretched out in front of me, as if to touch the outmost bounds of the universe. A great cosmic wind drives me. I have been freed from the law of gravity. But, soon, a cement weight invades my limbs. My heart is swollen, inexplicably, and my brain is slow! I fall back into hell, presumptuous Icarus – fallen angel remembering heaven. And in the Boeing 747 taking off from Montreal to Chicago, in the one taking off from Chicago to Los Angeles, and in the Boeing 747 that lifts off the runway of Los Angeles towards Honolulu, I tell myself everything that goes up must come down and that the number of take-offs and landings are generally identical.

'And how old is the captain?' the shaman asks abruptly, no doubt feeling my attention wavering. I automatically answer thirty-two. The orange cloudburst surrounded by the pink flames of Shiva's fire starts sliding on the green screen swelling like an ocean, spitting sea spray. It is the thirty-second card of the Dakini, that of Shiva, the Pillar of Fire. Superimposed on this moving image, we can now read: *All*

cause has an effect and all effect has a cause. It is the Sixth law of Mercury.

I go through the first thirty-two cards of the tantric Tarot mentally, and recognize the chain of cause and effect that has brought me here, today. I hear you, ma *belle* Yvelle, whispering: '*Trust your road map.*'

With a crackling more and more pronounced, the cathodic screen writes out: *Seventh Law of Mercury: All is androgynous.* Then the forty-seventh card of the Dakini appears, that of Playing Horses. An auburn pony in profile, head to the left, grazes on invisible grass on blue sand covered with a thin coat of water. Further, reflected in the blue mirror, three horses trot up. The one in the middle sports a pair of wings.

I see you again in your white silk suit, explaining that you are an androgyne Amazon angel, *belle* Yvelle. You play all roles in turn, you are as beautiful as a black vamp, as you are in chi-chi white, hiding behind your heart-shaped sunglasses.

The blue shaman takes my hands in hers. The room now bathes in a magenta glow that emanates from the ground. She looks into my eyes and sings:

Listen, listen to my heart song
Listen, listen to my heart song
I will never forget you
I will never forsake you
I will never forget you
I will never forsake you.

While I am singing with her, Time refracts our millennium meetings and catapults us to the place where our destinies wait.

An angel rises at the East window of my soul, as the lapping of waves on the black beach rock at *South Pacific* reminds me of the beach at Tulum in the Caribbean sea. I am eighteen years old and it is my wedding day. I am a Mayan woman for the third time already, and barely start to grasp the notion of time. I am twenty-seven years old, sightseeing in the Yucatan. I remember this.

The Caribbean sea is exactly the same blue. Cerulean. It is nonetheless incredible that through the millennium, blue has remained the same. Blue is a mystery. '*A little girl took me by the hand and made me run into the blue,*' said the stranger who meant *blé* (wheat). It was a Freudian slip and, yet, I remember. I wonder, ma *belle* Yvelle, if Miguel remembers.

VII

This Is My Body

I remember the mauve sun held between the palms of my hands, opened in the double mudra. I remember the fire of her breath on my forehead. I remember, Janice, I remember.

Pterophorous Nephthys, Egyptian goddess of the Louvre in Paris, flies over the crater of Mount Haleakala. Escaped from the funeral tank of Ramses III, this rose granite with a trace of polychrome from the twentieth dynasty is having fun kneeling on the rising sun of Maui, gold hieroglyph, symbol of durability. She slowly lifts her arms, gracefully letting her mauve wings fall. Goddess of the female sex, sister of Isis, the magician, Nephthys is herself a disconcerting hieroglyph. She prints the seal of reality on everything that she touches with her wings.

I know that it is her you are listening to, shaman, my love, while you are hammering the volcanic ground with your feet while singing:

> *I circle around*
> *I circle around*
> *The boundaries of the earth*

*Waving my long winged feathers
As I fly
Waving my long winged feathers
As I fly.*

You strike amethyst dust from the ground with your feet in a Sioux dance, connecting you to the fire burning at the centre of the earth. You spread out your red sleeves lined with violet silk, as if you really had wings. And while you are getting ready for your descent into the crater of the dead volcano, Amazon angels, androgynes, follow you in Indian file, beating the ground with their feet, unfurling imaginary wings that shine with morning dew. You are the head of this plumed serpent, shaman, my love. You are the head of this undulating serpent that winds along the slope of the crater.

I fidget with impatience, Janice. My whole consciousness is feet connected to this good old planet earth that spins in the cosmos. I am but one of the gleaming bracelets worn by the plumed serpent on the road towards the fire at the centre of the earth. I can feel its breath under the soles of my feet, climbing towards my legs, my sex, my belly, my stomach, my rib cage, my arms, my hands, my neck, my nape, my head. My spine is a cobra of gold whose large head levitates my skull, climbing to heaven, an ascent of Bengal's lights.

Saint Jean d'Acre, 1290. I am biting a juicy pomegranate. The nuggets explode in my mouth, releasing flavours of sun and sugar. I close my eyes on the essence of this favourite fruit.

Merlin would no doubt say that I am confusing the pleasure of pomegranate flesh and those, more mystical, of the quest for the Holy Grail. Does he not know that God is hiding in the loving flavour of this hellish fruit?

The caravansary exhales dust and oats, sweat and spices. I open my nostrils wide on the wind of humanity, blowing, carrying odours of frying and orange blossoms, of myrrh and manure. Merlin would surely laugh at me, accusing me, I, Théophilius Mistère, alchemist in the Crusade, of living in the odour of sanctity. Does he not know that the Holy Land can be, on a melancholic night, the stinking miasma of a messed-up transmutation?

The hospital bells are pealing. Their chimes vibrate my body, penetrating the fabric of my clothing; they probe the depths of my soul fallen asleep in the hollow of concern, and lift me in the ascending movement of pure exhilaration. Merlin would probably hiss if he heard me singing at the top of my lungs in the deserted Saint Jean d'Acre, on this grey Sunday morning. Does he not know that the Holy Ghost has just given me the gift of tongues?

My warm penis swells in my right hand. I feel it filling up with blood while fire tranfuses from the very depths of me. My heart is pounding, all my strength pulsing under tender skin, I explode, unctuous cream of sperm. Merlin would no doubt call me a cursed son of Onan. Does he not know that pleasure, a gift of God, is sacred?

The Mediterranean rolls blue up to the city and laps the white foam on the ochre ramparts. I look at the blue sky. Irresistibly my eyes go towards the fire of the sun at its zenith. My crystalline eyes attempt to focus on it but I must quickly close them. Violet incandescent spheres of divine intensity spin under my eyelids. Merlin would certainly assure me that my eyes are burning out. Does he not know that I have blind faith in that fire and that it is up to me to practise phosphenism?

A penetrating smell of rose reaches me. My ears ring. I place my hand on the rugged surface of the rampart, but I do not feel any texture. My hand goes through the rock that is but a particle of light in movement. An orange taste rises in my mouth. What is happening to me? An army of fierce Mamelukes is rushing towards Saint Jean d'Acre, now walking on water. Their scarlet banners float in the wind. I back off with dread.

It is then that Merlin appears from the clouds, above the Egyptian invaders. He is standing up, majestic as God the Father Himself. He is wearing a long, blue-velvet dress. His white hair floats around his mystical face, curiously flushed. I quickly understand. Merlin is furious with me. He brandishes an accusing finger and urges me from now on, to please keep my imaginary projections to myself. He swears that he has totally given up on the salvation of my soul. He explains that he is not my guardian angel, and no longer wants me as an apprentice if I persist in taking him for an imbecile.

I try cajoling him by asking what is the meaning, in his opinion, of the vision of the Mamelukes. He answers, furiously, that I should rather worry about my presence here. I then give him the nicest of my naive smiles, and tell him: 'But, Master, I was simply trying a new way of calling you!'

What is happening? A great wind lifts me from the ground and carries me away, spinning me in all directions, hurling me in a swirl of snow which is slowly falling in the blurred colours of an unfocused television screen. Someone adjusts the set.

A famous psychiatrist explains to the masses the difference between horizontal and vertical power. A hysterical young girl has agreed to participate in the program. She lies down on the couch, closes her eyes. She looks vulnerable and fragile. Her eyelids tremble ever so slightly. The psychiatrist sits in a comfortable armchair next to her, listening. She says, 'Tell me something.' He remains silent. She says again, 'Tell me something, please, tell me something.' He remains silent. She starts weeping. Her face contorts in pain, she bursts out in a shout. The man says, 'You are not pretty when you scream.' The young girl springs up, moves up to the camera and, as she tries to smile beneath the tears, says: 'I will now give you a demonstration of vertical power.'

She brandishes an axe above the head of the psychiatrist, deals him a blow in the middle of his skull. The automaton splits in two equal parts. In the left half of the android, a cassette recorder is still running. We only hear an unpleasant grinding on the nerves. On the other half, a black cloud of whirling smoke.

I then find myself crucified at the intersection of these horizontal and vertical powers. It is absolutely dark. I feel the walls of the room closing in around me.

Sticky hands try to grab me but the walls back off abruptly. Words squeak in the air, hum on my flesh like mosquitoes, sting momentum into my heart that jolts. I suffocate from the pain. I am streaming with sweat, and sink in despair. *'Eli, Eli, lema sabachthani.'*

It is then that I recall you, shaman, my love. In the black den at the borders of human suffering, I hear, feebly at first, then quite clearly, the echo of your voice, shaman, my love. *There is no other way but through.*

Tears of joy flow from my eyes, shaman, my love. I gently move my head to rock my pain. *There is no other way but through.* The music of Ravel's *Boléro* can now be heard. Music as red as my passion and sorrow. As I let my mind follow the energetic current of the *Boléro*, I notice that my limbs are no longer attached to me. The room floats in a diffused, red light. My essential beauty begins to dance in the alchemic hollow of death.

Bruce Lee suddenly jumps in front of me letting out a combat cry that freezes me on the spot. He appears to be in the middle of a karate film. After the first moment of astonishment has passed, I shout my ki-yi and let him have my right foot under the chin. He narrowly dodges the blow, retorts with a fatal palm blow on my nape. Luckily, I have the good sense to let myself fall flat on my belly, so that he strikes out in empty space. He loses his balance and also falls flat. I get up quickly to return to the position of attack. His eyes fulminate. The combat continues to the rhythms of our staccato breathing. The confrontation looks like a complex dance set to perfection. For one second, his attention yields. I take advantage of this and deal him a violent blow in the solar plexus. Choking, he is knocked down. He is fortunate that I used a soft technique. Had I weakened first, I do not doubt for one minute that he would have taken advantage of it and have knocked me down with a mortal blow. I hurry out before he can get onto his feet.

The sombre rhythm of the drum guides me through the night of my soul. I surrender totally to a spirit dancing in my body, shaking and tearing it apart. Possessed, I am possessed, shaman, my love. *There is a beast in the beat. There is a beast in the beat. There is a beast in the beat.*

I tumble down towards the centre of the volcano, Janice, light as a feather. Bouncing. Laughing, I spread out my imaginary angel wings. We are fifty Amazon angels, androgynes, hurtling down the slope following you, shaman, my love. Suddenly, halfway, you come to a halt. From the burning dawn sky, archangelic voices are like singing rain:

*I circle around
I circle around
The boundaries of the earth
Waving my long winged feathers
As I fly
Waving my long winged feathers
As I fly.*

Standing still on the slope of the volcano, we are looking at the plumed serpent being carried through the sky by Pterophorous Nephthys. Following her, delicately beating her white wings, the little snow maiden by Joseph Cornell. Behind her, a half-naked go-go boy in black boots sways his hips in a completely mystical way. Follows Loie Fuller, a rustling of orchid-coloured veils, Nijinsky and several acrobats from the Peking Opera. Isadora Duncan, wearing a lilac tunic, balances her long arms with quivering hands. Behind her are ten little boys and girls in Greek tunics and sandals. And, closing off the march, majestic in her white and blue cotton dress and her halo of white hair, Agatha Christie. The aging lady is surrounded by Dickie, Dickmistress and Lord Tony, invisible playmates from her childhood.

It is funny, Janice, how all of a sudden, Agatha Christie looks like my grandmother.

In the aerial space between Honolulu and Maui, an air stewardess from Aloha Airlines in an orange-tang coloured muumuu brings a sealed envelope addressed to me. Surprised, I ask her what it is about. She smiles, raises her shoulders, and leaves. I open the envelope. I find, hastily scribbled, the following message:

> *Creo recordar que fué tan grande mi saombro que empecé a tratar a la maquina de 'usted'. Antes de marchar dije a mi jefe: 'No podré nunca tocar esta maquina. Esta maquina es para mi como un superior jera quico, como un delegado de Hacienda o un director general. Comprendo que no lograré olvidarla nunca y que hablaré siempre de ella a mis amigos.'*

I cannot help smiling at the thought that Miguel seems convinced I will succeed in decoding his message even though he gives me no clues to decipher it.

From the bottom of the volcanic basin, dark and solemn, I see Montreal, fuchsia town turning city of violets and lilacs, in the magnetic heart of the love archangel. Montreal, Janice, descends slowly into the crater, opening her Amazon angel wings.

VIII

Imagine

The sunrise, red, in the mauve dawn of Montreal. I write Estelle, all the violet night singing in her. I write Valentina, amber of rose indigo. I write Iris, blue pearl in the rainbow memory. I write Viviane, green Vivi solipsist. I write Andjela, in gold; Yvelle, orange of angel of gold; I write Janice, red passion. They are spinning, bionic, a rainbow every three minutes, in the mists of time of things.

They are spinning and blending in the white of the eyes of the Amazon angel, snowing in the heart of springtime in Acadia. On the road between Caraquet and Moncton, I look for colours in the snowy landscape. Kneeling in the back seat, nose glued against the window, I am looking for red. I find garages, a truck, a bedspread on a clothesline, two cars, a barn roof decorated with a moosehead. I am looking for orange, yellow, and I find cars, sweaters, skirts. I find yellow posts, traffic lights, trucks, a Shell garage sign. All road signs are green, so are the trees, the houses. The sky is blue, rivers, cars, houses. Navy blue, the sea, in the distance. Mauve, mauve is much rarer.

I am going to miss you, archangel Gabriel. The holocaust will not have happened in vain. Not knowing how to love you has taught me to love. You have changed my course on the locus of time, you have turned my head around, archangel Gabriel. I have wandered for centuries in the labyrinths of time, inhabited by tigers and jaguars. Each one of our meetings has been painful to me in the mists of time. I bid you adieu now, archangel Gabriel. Adieu, I love you, but adieu.

To the air of *Indigo* by Peter Gabriel on the radio, the powder-blue Chevelle turns towards Moncton. On the road sign above the highway: Scoudouc. As in *Mourir à Scoudouc* by Herménégilde Chiasson.

Gérald Leblanc has opened a bar in Cancun. It is called *The Mists of Time*. Philippe Aubert de Gaspé fils works in the cloakroom and Jean-Paul Daoust is barman. Anaïs Nin, standing at the bar, is chatting with Lucien Francoeur disguised as Tutankhamon. Severo Sarduy as a Tibetan monk and Hubert Aquin in a bowler hat are playing a pinball machine. Nicole Brossard is explaining the function of holography to a very interested Doris Lessing. Paul Chamberland is demonstrating his writing computer to Agatha Christie and a group of Mayan children. Incognito behind his heart-shaped sunglasses, Claude Beausoleil declares with conviction: '*Liber aperit librum*', which means 'The book opens the book'. Gabrielle Roth arrives in a gust and announces that she has just completed the writing of *The Dancing Path: A Shamanic Way to Ecstasy.*

I am going to miss you, archangel Raphael. Standing on the roof of the RCA Building in New York, in December. I look at heavy dark clouds amassing on the horizon. Thousands of people are gathered this afternoon in Central Park to mourn John Lennon. The snow starts from the end of the horizon and falls in gusts on New York. Eight million, ten million souls? The flash of light from the Hudson, the bouquet of green of Central Park, of Washington Square. Grey. Dark grey everywhere. New York today, December 14th, 1980, is a black city in memory of the rock'n'roll archangel. I am going to miss your music, archangel Raphael, who remembers heaven so well.

When the ultimate black phosphene turns off, there is only the black of the black left, isn't it so, Miguel? '*Negro de negro.*' I am going to miss you, archangel Michael. You nimbly handle the net used to catch the soft water serpent that springs to the side of your red canoe, on the post card 'Original

Photocopy Art', by Amy Wilson, 1979. You are fluttering above the water in your green armour, your mauve cape. Around your fairness, a red halo. Yellow on green background, in the water, these words: *Suppressing the demon within him.* I am going to miss you, archangel Michael. I am going to miss you.

Ah Lucifer, Lucifer, for the beauty of the devil I have been in hell. The Amazon angel extends her arms, takes me towards ten thousand suns turning at the end of the sky.

But it is on earth and in this solar system that I will find you again Miguel, my soul. In dreams, your hair is very black, your name is Ramon, you live, I believe, in Buenos Aires, and you stink of alcohol. Your wife releases the chaffinches, as if by accident, at every one of my visits. It is always a bother finding them again. You speak English, in any case, because the last time, you told me: '*What I feel, you can feel too, isn't it?*'

Evidently, I am not controlling my dreams very well at the moment. I would very much prefer that you would not be drunk when I go join you at the other end of the world. When we embark on the *Navire Night,* Miguel, it is to dream with precision. Since you have been my guide in China, since Amélie, since you have been my wife in Hawaii, my lover in Paris, my granddaughter, my man, Christiane V. in Germany, my Mayan torturer, the Great Inquisitor, my Merlin, I search for you frantically every time. This time, consciously. Wishing you to be conscious also, while the Amazon angel reunites us in front of an extraordinary sunset.

Imagine, Miguel, imagine for just a moment what will time be if we learn to move through it at will. Imagine, imagine, Miguel, what will space be if the violet flame clarifies it and we can, finally, inhabit it in peace. Imagine, Miguel, imagine for just one moment what will the species be if the memory comes back, Miguel, if the memory comes back.

I see you writing in pink neon letters on the black wall of your studio, Miguel. I see you writing: *Dream.* I picture you, chameleon shaman, double of my rainbow soul rising in the pink quartz of the visual archangel. I picture you unpredictable and possible, incarnate, of fire.

I dream you are there, Miguel. I simply picture you there, real. I softly transpose in the oasis of mirages, for we must be careful with mirages. I will go softly in my belly dance of a thousand-and-one nights that I do not wish to repeat, Miguel, that I certainly do not wish to repeat.

It is the beginning of the world. I am gliding in a canoe towards Hochelaga. It is autumn. It is sunny, very sunny. I am the great chief Ottawa en route towards Hochelaga. The water is so calm that the banks of the Saint Lawrence are reflected as in a brilliant mirror. They give us mirrors in exchange for a territory. They give us mirrors on which our images are reflected while the ground slips under our feet. I glide on the frozen waters of the Saint Lawrence, happy, unhappy, good times, bad times. All of this, after all, is of little importance. Time is a circle, I inhabit a circle. My people are circular. They give us mirrors so we will think differently. They give us mirrors to deprive us of a territory. This water is good to drink. This land abounds with game. Why do they value so much the creation of boundaries? They give us mirrors so that we will not see what they are doing to our territory. They give us mirrors to render us illusory. My canoe enters the Hochelaga archipelago, gleaming in the flamboyant gold of October. The colour red climbs trees like the red blood that flows in our veins. Hochelaga bursts open, orange, ochre, crimson, rose through the remains of green, on the blue and indigo of the sky.

Remember, Miguel, remember Atlantis. Imagine the return of our race to the earth,

Miguel. Let the Amazon angel awaken the circuits of your memory and enter Montreal, Montreal, city of many colours. Montreal, Montreal, mirror archangel remembering Indian summer.

Printed by
Ateliers Graphiques Marc Veilleux Inc.
Cap-Saint-Ignace (Québec)
in August 1993